BRYONY ROSEHURST

Kiss of Death

Content Warnings

- Death, blood, violence, and strong language
- Medium to high heat, with scenes of a sexual nature
- Body scarring and trauma
- An attempt at self-harm born from Maeve's confusion of her own physical form in the afterlife
- "Monsters"/reanimated corpses

Chapter One

If there was not a Pret A Manger in perfect view just up the road, Maeve Grey might have believed she'd traveled back in time. As it was, she tilted her shield-maiden helmet over her right eye to pretend the popular coffee shop did not sit on the corner of the cobbled Shambles, focusing instead on the wooden huts and stalls selling Norse-themed goods. She loved York's Viking Week; the medieval buildings, narrow streets, and tall cathedrals were the perfect setting to get lost in as her tough alter-ego, Brunhild, especially when most visitors seemed to wish for the same in their roughspun tunics and leather armor. It was like Comic-Con for history lovers.

Of course, minus the modern cafe chains, there was also India's sea-blue hair to drag Maeve back to reality. Together, they set out India's handmade jewelry on her collapsible table: dangly gold earrings with a colourful array of gemstones and crystals, pendants shaped like daggers, brooches in the shape of longships.

Maeve tutted at the very sight. "I'm so jealous of your talent." She had spent much of her money on India's beautiful creations over the years and couldn't compliment them enough.

India rolled her eyes. She hadn't dressed up much for the occasion, wearing a rainbow-striped slouchy cardigan and high-waisted mom jeans. Where Maeve went all out, India chose comfort — and Maeve couldn't blame her, because her own linen costume was awfully scratchy and a bit too thick for a clammy July.

"You have plenty of talents!"

"Like?" Maeve asked.

India set out her price sheets, clearly stalling. "Like... being Brunhild?"

If only Maeve's ability to dress up and perform in battle reenactments was an employable skill. At the moment, she couldn't find a job for the life of her, and her long-term relationship had ended not a month before. She had labelled this her quarter-life crisis, by which she meant she was hoping that a massive fissure would spread across the ground of York and swallow her whole so she wouldn't have to figure out what came next. She didn't like starting her life again at twenty-six. She'd never been all that good at existing in the first place, really, always feeling slightly behind the curve.

At least helping India with her business kept her busy. Maeve was currently her friend's personal postwoman, making trips to the post office twice a day to send out Etsy orders. It only paid in spare coins and cups of tea but it eased Maeve's guilt about sleeping on India's couch with Loki the cat every night, having recently moved out of her ex-girlfriend's place with nowhere else to go.

"Great," she muttered flatly, arranging a collection of rings on India's mannequin hand. She was sick of feeling bad about herself for reaching a dead end in her life, but she couldn't seem to shake herself out of the pity party this time.

India sighed and put a comforting hand on Maeve's shoulder. "You'll find something. It'll work out in the end."

It was easy to say for someone with passion and direction. India had a long-distance fiancée who she planned on moving to Glasgow with soon and she'd earned enough from making jewellery that she no longer needed a day job. Maeve couldn't help but wonder when her life might work out that way. When would she get to the good part?

But she wouldn't mope today. Stoic shield-maiden Brunhild had bigger things to worry about — she had a battle reenactment to get to. After quickly rebraiding her fishtail plait and slipping her round helmet back onto her head, Maeve bid India goodbye and collected her wooden sword and shield from beneath the table before marching away with her chin held high.

If it wobbled just slightly, nobody noticed.

* * *

The reenactment took place in the gardens of the Yorkshire Museum with a set of arching Roman ruins as their backdrop. Maeve had stopped plenty of times along the way as families asked to take pictures of her, most likely because of the dark yet elegant warrior makeup India had laboured over this morning. Hundreds of people were ready and waiting, so many that she couldn't even begin to search for the few friends she'd met over the years. She slipped into the crowd, finding her audience as big as ever behind the rope that cordoned the battle from the spectators. She didn't know what it was about reenactments, but they seemed to carry electric anticipation through the air as though real blood was about to be shed.

Thank God it wasn't. Brunhild might have been brutal, but Maeve much preferred safety and comfort over violence.

3

In fact, she didn't have much Viking in her at all minus the costume.

Maybe one day she'd find her fight, but today she only had to pretend.

Their signal to begin came in the form of a well-rehearsed speech between the two warriors leading their armies. They were fighting over a settlement, with Maeve's group the invaders and the others defending their Viking village. Sometimes, she liked being the villain of the story, the one who acted first — even if she often got lost in the back with her short stature and lacklustre sword.

As the unclear dialogue scattered into the wind, the movement began. One hundred shouts tangled through the air as they readied their weapons and shields. Maeve's eyes narrowed instinctively and she gripped her sword as though it was another limb, part of her. She was a shield-maiden now, brave and fierce and poised. When the claxon sounded and the two armies rushed like tides to make one fierce tempest, Maeve went with them, sending out whacks and stabs where wood clattered raucously against wood. Everything was drowned out by that sound. It rattled through her bones and emptied her brain of any thoughts, any fear, any self-doubt.

Brunhild sent several Vikings flying as she filed away at the army, yelling and feigning pain when needed for the sake of the engrossed viewers. Children gasped. Parents laughed. One man tried to spear her; she deflected with her shield, face contorting into something between a grimace and a grin as her sword sang through the air and landed, lightly, on his shoulder. The reenactor collapsed to the ground, pretending to nurse his wounds, and she felt as proud as a real champion.

Confident now, she decided to show off, using footwork she'd

4

learned from television shows and slipping her way around her attackers like the fast-footed predator Brunhild was. She fell into swordplay with another woman, their weapons clashing in the air to form a cross. She was driven back for a moment, but Brunhild was more clever than her adversary and deflected the sword with her shield while plunging her own between the woman's armpit and arm.

The woman sank to the floor with a slightly over-the-top scream before whispering, "You go, girl!" with a clandestine high five.

Maeve gave it to her, grinning before continuing on. Sweat poured from her helmet, no doubt smudging the makeup around her eyes. It didn't help that the midday sun had crawled slowly from the clouds and now dazzled her. She squinted, trying to ward off the next silhouette launching at her—

Something sharp and burning roared through her gut. She put it down to a stitch at first and attempted to ward away the woman with her sword. But the woman was smirking and the pain was getting worse.

The pointy, metal tip of her spear was covered in blood.

Alarmed and nauseous, she looked down and fell to her knees. Blood soaked her thin leather armor, a hole fraying the material just above her belly button. She was injured.

The reenactment had just gotten a little bit too real.

Panic thundered through her as the woman ran away, weaving through crowds until Maeve lost sight of her. Maeve shouted for help but her voice was lost in the mangled screams of the reenactors feigning bloody deaths on the ground. They thought she was part of the act. For a moment, Maeve convinced herself it was too, but when she tried to push herself back to her feet, her knees gave out and her energy seemed to drain from her all at once.

She hit the grass with a thud, the smell of damp soil the last thing she remembered before the voices ebbed and the world went dark.

Chapter Two

The Goddess of Death ripped through the wind, clutching the leather reins of her three-legged mount, Helhest — or Hester when Hel was being affectionate. Hester's hooves pounded across the thatched golden arch of Gjallarbrú, soaring over the river Gjöll and tearing through the veil that separated the living from the dead. The permanent from the temporary.

She had a new soul to claim; could feel it thrumming in her hot blood and cold bones. They called to her, though Hel couldn't quite distinguish who "they" were. She would have to get closer, and all the while hope it wasn't a pathetic old soul taken from a disease-riddled body. They were usually the whiny ones, and Hel didn't have time for whiny today.

Glittering gold turned to fertile soil and wild, trampled grass as Hel spurred Hester with a heavy-booted nudge to her side. She waved at her guard, Modgud, on her way, and Modgud waved back as the wind Hel left behind her rippled through her dark hair.

And then, without warning, Hester's steadfast, muscular body began to topple beneath Hel's saddle.

No, it wasn't Hester who was trembling. It was the ground beneath her hooves. Hel risked a glance over her shoulder, a harsh frown burrowing into her half-flesh, half-shadow-swallowed forehead. Hekla's snow-capped mountain peak pierced the low, gray clouds beyond Gjallarbrú, the road to Helheim no longer visible. No, it was shrouded by smog, and Hekla... Hekla was spitting out inky plumes of smoke.

She hadn't seen it at first, not with her vision shaking from the jostling of Hester's uneven canters. A dread she had not felt in eons feasted on her gristly insides. Something was wrong with Hekla. Her wispy clouds painted everything black. And the ice... the ice was trembling with the rest of the craggy mountain, tumbling down, its grip slipping.

Everything was slipping. Hel could feel it now. Though her grasp on Hester's reins remained tight, something oily and quaking had gathered her in its arms and was shaking her about. A guttural howl ripped through the world. Garmr's, her hellhound.

Is something happening at the gates?

"Turn back!" she ordered her granite-black steed, her shout a bellowing rumble of thunder that rent through the collapsing world. "Turn back, Helhest!"

But Hester continued stoically as the smoke chased and choked them — until Hel was engulfed by a foggy blue night from which there was no escape.

She continued on, a hundred dazzling and motley-coloured lights disorientating her. Hel gritted her teeth against sudden thunder and rain as she tried to catch her bearings.

Where are we? she wondered, panic rising.

"Hester!" Hel yelled, her one eye darting frantically around in its shadowed socket. "Hester, go back!"

Wherever they were, it wasn't pleasant. They were surrounded by towering blocks of stone on all sides, all of them pouring with golden lights. She looked up, searching for the stars, but could find none. This wasn't her world. So what was it?

Hel didn't have a chance to find out. Hester rose onto a new pathway—

And then Hel felt it.

They were still calling. The person she had come to collect, still waiting. Whatever predicament she'd fallen into in this land of lights and crowded stone would have to be figured out later.

Despite the horse's bewilderment, Hester knew where to take Hel. The horse heard the callings as Hel did, knew what needed to be done. She could feel fate's thread winding tighter the closer they got. They turned a corner, crossing a set of dashed lines painted thickly on the road. *What are these strange markings?*

She continued on, trusting Hester and the Norns, the Fates, to guide her to the fallen. Through archways and cobbled roads, narrow streets barely big enough to accommodate Hel's broad shoulders.

Finally, they reached an open, grassy terrain. Hester's hooves sunk into the soil, barely dodging splinters of wood and what looked to be poorly whittled wooden swords. And there... was that a boot?

It had been a brutal battle, then, though she saw no warriors. Only the fallen one that Hel had come to claim, crumpled on the trampled grass in blood-soaked armor.

The warrior's eyes fluttered open at the sound of Hester's heavy hooves, face sallow and drawn. Hel was relieved, for at least this mortal, a woman wearing leather and linen as any respecting skjaldmær, shield-maiden, would, was from the

9

world Hel knew. She was not lost after all. Perhaps she was just further south than she was used to.

Or so she thought, until the skjaldmær's fading spirit hopped from the floor, leaving behind her lifeless body.

"Shit!" she exclaimed, bringing a trembling hand to her blood-congealed forehead. "What the *fuck* is going on?"

That sharp-edged language wasn't Norse. Hel detected a few English words among the curses and understood well enough from her vast experience. Still, it wasn't how a warrior usually greeted her goddess, her lips curled in distaste. She looked behind her at the unfamiliar landscape, wondering how far away they were from Hekla and whether her mountain remained in one piece. She needed to get back and wasn't quite sure where to start.

She would have to give the short version then, which suited her just fine. She was tired of delivering speeches of the afterlife by now, anyway — though she only ever had to for those who refused to believe that the gods existed. She grunted, dismounting from Hester and crossing her arms over her large chest.

"You are dead."

The shield-maiden stiffened, her eyes so wide they seemed to be escaping her skull. She looked down again at her body and let out a sound Hel had never heard before.

It sounded an awful lot like a sob.

* * *

Maeve gawked down at her own body, nothing more than a bloody, pale heap on the grass. *This can't be real. It isn't real!* How could she be both here and there, dead and not? Were there two of her? Was this what people meant when they spoke of out-of-body experiences?

Her hands rose to her stomach, where she remembered the spear point tearing through her flesh. The weapon was no longer there, but congealed blood stained her thin, frayed "armour." Perhaps she shouldn't have chosen the cheap leather-like material when making her costume — but how was she to know somebody would come at her with a real, pointy spear?

Did they?

Surely not. She was dreaming, or maybe hallucinating. Perhaps the blueberry muffin she'd eaten this morning had been laced with something. Could someone have spiked her coffee? Did she even drink coffee? Her mind jumbled with a million different questions until she swayed on her feet, dizzy. She peeled her eyes from the dead version of her, finding the giant woman glaring at her impatiently. Tall and brawny, she wasn't any better to look at beneath her hood. The right side of her face was normal, full of colour, with a near-black iris and plump pink lips. But the flesh tapered off and left only bone on the left side, as though somebody had torn away half of her face. Exposed bone and sinew were left behind, like some sort of elaborate Halloween mask.

Only it wasn't a mask. When she spoke, the fleshless mouth moved. When she blinked, it was only out of her one-lidded eye — the other a hollow socket.

It wasn't real. Because if this was real, if Maeve was really dead and this creature was staring at her, made of colour and decay, that meant she might be in Hell. And Maeve didn't believe in Hell. Maeve didn't *belong* in Hell. She was a jobless bisexual, yes, and perhaps she'd stolen sweets from the post office once or twice as a teen, but she'd never done anything bad enough to deserve this; to deserve a spear through her, to deserve this strange, dark world.

York looked as though it had been draped in a sheer veil. She could make out the cathedral and church spires pointing toward the rich-purple sky, but it felt as though somebody had tried to hide the details. Dark clouds lingered above, a steady buzz of static humming through the air as though a storm was on its way.

Nausea churned through her and she braced her hands against her knees, trying to catch her breath as the ground spun beneath her feet. "It isn't real," she repeated over and over again. "None of this is real."

"On the contrary." The giantess leaned tiredly against her tall sceptre as though bored. It also seemed to be made of bone, matching her eerily exposed skull, and thinned into two razor-sharp points at the top. A crescent moon with deadly edges. "You have simply reached the next stage in your journey, Skjaldmær." A heavy hand was laid between Maeve's shoulder blades and Maeve had to fight not to stumble. She was strong, this woman, standing at least two feet taller than Maeve's five-foot-one stature. "Hel awaits."

"*Hell?*" Maeve shot up, blanching. "No! No, I can't go to Hell! I don't belong in Hell!" The reenactor who had killed her and then walked away... *she* belonged in Hell. Bad people belonged in Hell. Maeve... Maeve wasn't a bad person. Was she?

"Please." Tears sprang to her eyes as she clasped her hands together in a plea. "Please. I'm not ready. I'm not ready to die."

She looked down at her body again and began to crumble as she thought of all the movies she hadn't watched yet, all the songs she hadn't listened to. The concert tickets still on the dresser of her ex's house because she hadn't been brave enough to go and get them back after the breakup. And what about the rest of her life? She wanted to fall in love again. She wanted a nice house and a job she enjoyed. She wanted to visit Thailand and Egypt and go back to Venice. She wanted to take more grainy photographs of blazing sunsets on her iPhone.

She wanted more.

"Get up," she willed the other version of her, the dead version of her. But her frame remained still, eyes closed and blood crusted at the corners of her mouth. "Get *up!*" she shouted.

"Skjaldmær...." The woman squeezed her shoulder now, causing Maeve to wince. Her fist was crushing, whether she meant it to be or not, and she yanked herself away as fear climbed up her throat.

The woman's one visible eye glistened like onyx, her eyebrow cocked in confusion as she took a wary step away. "Don't you know who I am?"

Maeve shook her head, swallowing thickly. Was she supposed to? Was it a test? She was failing royally if it was. But she couldn't say she knew many people who looked like the behemoth, mangled woman in front of her. She was the stuff of nightmares, horror stories, her dark matted hair swirling around her as though it didn't wish to touch her; as though it wasn't brave enough to. A crown circled her brow, made up of thorns that seemed to dig into her mottled skin. No, Maeve didn't know who this woman was. She could only guess her to be a demon here to drag her to Hell.

Thunder rumbled without warning, startling Maeve.

Hel looked around curiously, fist turning white around her sceptre. "Where is this place?" Hel asked. "Where am I?"

Maeve didn't know how to answer that, still trembling, still terrified.

"Answer me, Skjaldmær!" Her voice boomed without warning, louder than the storm itself, and Maeve stumbled back as though she'd been struck.

"York!" Maeve cried. "You're in York!"

"*York*," Hel repeated, wandering around the grass. Her horse whinnied as though growing impatient, its coat so black it shined blue as a raven's feathers. Maeve blinked as she looked at it properly, finding only one leg in the center of its chest rather than the usual two. And there, bone jutted just the same as it did in the woman's face. Ribs. Maeve could see its ribs.

Another bout of terror dropped in her stomach and left her breathless. The woman turned her back and Maeve inched further away. Slowly at first. When her movement went unnoticed, a surge of adrenaline rushed through her. She set off into a run, heading for the city walls, for anywhere but here.

She wasn't going to Hell today.

The demon would have to catch her first.

Chapter Three

The sound of hoofs striking stone followed Maeve through York, her lungs burning as she ran as quickly as her untrained legs would allow. It was difficult. The city she had lived in since the age of eighteen no longer felt familiar, the thick blue veil seeming to have changed everything. Streets she couldn't remember ever seeing before, empty of shops as though they were only a cheap mimic of her home. She passed through shadows that made her blood run cold, but finally, finally, reached the main road.

It was empty. No cars went by, no pedestrians wandered the streets.

She felt as though she were underwater, her ears too full to hear anything but her own pulse. Frantically, she crossed the River Ouse, which was nothing more than a slithering black serpent that reflected nothing, held nothing — just like the demon's eyes. Relief filled her when she finally turned the corner onto Moss Street, where India's blue door faced a primary school, just as it always had.

She was home, and she could no longer hear the horse chasing her. Perhaps it had all been a dream — perhaps, any moment, she would wake up on the couch with Loki tucked into her side. Stumbling through the garden gate, she tried the door. It gave easily under her fingers but she didn't have time to worry about why that might be, because India often felt paranoid that any old weirdo might walk in and so kept her doors locked. Tripping over shoes by the doormat, she burst into the living room...

And found it empty.

"*India?*" she screamed, pacing from the living room to the kitchen before sprinting up the stairs two at a time. Her thighs burned and she felt shaky, as though she might faint. "India!"

The bedroom was in darkness, and the bathroom, too. India wasn't there. Where was she?

A sob fell from Maeve and she used the doorjamb for support, sucking in deep breaths, trying to steady her racing heart. *This isn't real. It's just a dream.*

She just needed to wake up.

In the bathroom, she tried to run the cold tap in an effort to splash her face. But her hands passed straight through the star-shaped handle, through skin and veins and tendons, and Maeve didn't feel any of it.

She straightened, wondering if she was a ghost. But she'd felt tired and achy when she'd been running. She'd felt a breeze, felt the humidity of a coming storm. Rain dappled her skin, mingling with sweat and leaving her shiny. Ghosts couldn't sweat, could they?

She turned on the light and looked in the mirror. Her own face stared back, thank goodness, though it was stained green and red, grass and blood. The warrior make-up India had painted on this morning was smeared, making her look dirty, and the Viking helmet still balanced on her head, hair slipping out of their braids. She still looked like Maeve. She still recognized her reflection.

So why had her body been crumpled on the grass? Why couldn't she turn on the tap?

A loud clunk echoed up the stairs and Maeve's chin trembled with fear.

She'd been found.

Without thinking, she turned off the light and hid in the bath, pulling the shower curtain around her. Just in time, too. A heavy set of footsteps thundered up the stairs in time with the storm outside, in time with Maeve's pounding heart. She squeezed her eyes shut, curling her knees to her chest and praying—

The shower curtain was ripped back, and there was the demon. As she snarled, Maeve realised she wasn't waking up.

This wasn't a dream.

"Hello again, Skjaldmær," the demon said.

Maeve screamed.

* * *

Hel was growing impatient with the shield-maiden. The chase through the strange new setting of light, square buildings, and winding roads had proven she was very far from home, and the newness of it all left her uneasy. She was used to bloody battles, rolling Scandinavian hills, and wintry planes. She was used to the comfort of her underworld, her gilded dark rooms, and her land of peace where warriors rested and celebrated.

She was not used to mortals screaming in her face as though they could think of no worse fate than joining her; than passing through her gates and being granted the comfort of an afterlife. She was beginning to wonder if sending the woman to Niflheim wasn't a better option.

"*Enough!*" Hel bellowed, thrusting her sceptre into the ground and leaving behind a crack.

The shield-maiden flinched further into herself, covering her face with her trembling hands. "Please. Don't. Please don't hurt me."

Hel stopped, her brows pinching together. If this wasn't her world, perhaps the woman truly did not know who Hel was. But that was impossible. Hel had seen the aftermath of the battle: the blood and the torn armor. She'd seen the weapons. And the shield-maiden still wore her helmet, dented as it was. Never had a soul called out for her and led to this. Hel always knew. It was her job to know. To listen to the souls and choose the ones who belonged with her in the underworld. The Norns had led her here for a reason.

They must have.

The fear rolling off the mortal made Hel uncomfortable. She may have enjoyed scaring those unworthy, those headed for the horrors of Niflheim when their judgment came, but warriors deserved better. Her job was to bring them peace. Or, rather, bring them *to* peace.

Even so, she was not accustomed to being... *kind*. She'd never had reason to care about people's emotions before now. Most of those she encountered were just grateful to have been greeted by the goddess as they passed on. She did her job efficiently, and that was what mattered. How on Midgard was she to calm somebody in a panic?

She supposed dropping her bone sceptre would be a start. Reluctantly, Hel propped it by a strange-looking washbasin and blew out a frustrated breath that rattled through the room. The woman flinched again.

"I'm not here to hurt you," Hel said finally. "You needn't be

18

afraid." She lowered her hood, her black cape rippling across the tiles and the hilt of her sheathed sword jutting into her hip.

The shield-maiden peeked at Hel between her hands, tentative.

Hel sighed and folded her arms, leather armour creaking with the movement. "You should be honoured I came for you. Is this how all warriors of your kind act?" She sniffed, unable to hide her disapproval. If this snivelling, scared woman in front of her was a warrior, it was no wonder she had lost her life today. Hel could not imagine her in the underworld among brave, fierce fighters who had never shown an ounce of fear, even in death. "You disappoint me, Skjaldmær."

"I'm not a warrior," the woman whispered. "And my name isn't... 'Skelmur.'"

Hel ran her tongue across her half-exposed teeth with more than a little agitation. Did this woman truly not understand anything? "You are a shield-maiden. That is what skjaldmær means."

"But I'm not." She shook her head adamantly, unfolding herself slowly from her ball in the porcelain tub. "This is only a costume."

She took off her helmet, revealing unnaturally silver hair that seemed to darken at the roots. Her pale features and ice-blue eyes might have been mistaken for Icelandic, only her face was smooth. Youthful. She didn't look as though she'd been roughened by the harsh northern winds or scarred by brutal battles — minus her bloody, torn armor. She looked unscathed, as though she'd only just begun her fight rather than ended it.

"I wasn't in a real battle today. It was a reenactment. It was supposed to be pretend. But somebody... a woman... her spear went right through me." Her voice was nothing more than a whisper, broken by the threat of tears. Her watery eyes met Hel's. "I'm not a shield-maiden, and I'm not supposed to be here. I'm not supposed to die."

For a moment, Hel's chest burned with the fear that she was telling the truth. But what sort of world was this, where battles were nothing but pretend?

She glanced around again, distaste curling across her face. "And where is 'here?' Where are we if not Midgard?"

"Midgard...?" The girl looked puzzled and Hel wondered why the language of her own words was causing such issues now. Skjaldmær. Midgard. Perhaps it was even why she was so afraid of Helheim.

Because she didn't know.

"Earth," Hel supplied carefully, raising an eyebrow. "The realm of humans."

Unless...

Had she stumbled into a new, undiscovered realm? But that would be impossible. For years, Yggdrasil, the world tree, had unified the nine realms with its great branches. Connected Helheim to Midgard, Midgard to Asgard, where the gods resided.

She thought of the black smoke. The trembling ground. Hekla's anguish as Hel rode away from the gates. Could that have caused some sort of collapse? Some... alternative to everything Hel knew?

And if that was true, what was to become of her home? Of all her people in Helheim who were just trying to find peace after life?

She'd left them behind in the midst of chaos.

Her blood turned cold. They were her responsibility and she was not there. Stupidly, she had gotten herself lost. More focused on an insignificant mortal than the destruction of her own land. *Why did Helhest and the Norns bring me here?*

None of it made sense, and yet the unease kept crawling across her bones like spiders.

"This is Earth," the mortal whispered. "I am human."

But it wasn't Hel's Earth. She wasn't supposed to be here. Narrowing her eyes, she stepped to examine the girl more closely. She crouched in front of the bathtub, reaching out in asking with the hand covered in flesh. Not everybody took to the other half of her.

Slowly, eyes filled with wild lightning, the mortal nodded. Permission. Hel drew closer, tracing the shape of the woman's face as gently as she knew how. It was rare her hands were used for anything other than wielding her sceptre or clutching Hester's reins — she had forgotten what another person's warm skin felt like. The mortal's was clammy and silken, though not without its bumps, scars, and freckles. Half of her pale complexion was smudged with war paint, her hair matted to a forehead not yet creased by maturity. Her jawline was round, soft, as though she'd lived a life full of comfort and good food rather than war and hunger. The woman's eyes fluttered shut. Such a human reaction.

She *was* human, and yet... she was right. She was no warrior. Bore no scars or calluses, no sign of struggle. Hel focused on her neck then, searching for a pulse. The ghost of a heartbeat no longer needed fluttered against Hel's fingertips, more telling of her enduring spirit than her physical state. She'd always thought it strange, the way her warriors' souls still danced with life even when they had abandoned their mortal bodies. It was part of their call, part of the reason they were deemed worthy. Some spirits were empty without a physical presence, while others lived on boldly.

As this one was. Further proof that Hel had been meant to find her. This woman was made to be claimed in Helheim.

Her throat bobbed and Hel let her hand drop to her side. "I have never met a human like you before. You claim not to be a warrior and yet a drum beats in you all the same."

"I don't know what that means," the woman admitted.

"What is your name?" Hel asked, her armour rustling as she stood. The top of her head grazed the ceiling.

"Maeve."

"Maeve," Hel repeated. She had never heard that name before, she spent another moment scrutinizing all that was strange and new. *Fascinating.* "My name is Hel. I am the goddess of death. Would you perhaps consider getting out of that tub now, Maeve? It seems we have some things to speak about."

Maeve hesitated, her white-knuckled grip clenching slightly around the porcelain rim of the bath.

"Am I really dead?" Her voice shook, the words barely audible.

Something foreign ran down Hel's throat. Regret? Sympathy? Why should she feel such things? She was here to help.

"Death is only something that happens to a mortal being," she explained. "Your body is dead, yes, but your spirit lives on. That's how you remain here."

Maeve squeezed her eyes shut. When she opened them, her lashes were damp and her irises limned with the same sharp strength as a steel blade. Warrior, through and through — even if she didn't know it.

She rose slowly out of the tub. Hel extended her hand to help her out and she took it with caution before climbing down. That gentle warmth returned.

22

"Okay," Maeve said. "Let's talk."

Chapter Four

Maeve led the woman who called herself Hel into India's living room, the sound of thudding boots following her through the corridor and stopping in time with Maeve. She felt out of place. India's home had always felt like hers, too. Yes, her crumpled duvet had been shoved in the corner of the couch where she'd left it in a rush to leave this morning, but...

There was a quiet now she had never felt before, filling her ears like wax. It wasn't quite silence. She could hear the steady rise and fall of Hel's breaths, and her own, but the usual hum of the refrigerator seemed not to reach her the way it had so many nights before when she had slept in this room, on that couch. Outside, it was pitch-black. The street lamps were unlit and every terraced house was in darkness. She caught a moving shadow by the window — then realized it was Hel's ghostly three-legged horse outside. Waiting to bring her to her fate, perhaps. Maybe she was a fool to keep fighting it.

She collapsed onto the couch, watching Hel carefully. Hel watched back, her face broken by shadows but not quite as merciless as it had been in the Museum Gardens. It had surprised Maeve when she'd reached out with that enormous hand and touched her so gently. She still felt the aftershocks like frost thawing across her skin.

"This doesn't feel like my world either," Maeve began. "It's the same, but not. It's so dark here. Is this…" — she gulped — "is it because I'm dead?" The word sliced her tongue like a knife through flesh, coming out serrated and splintered. *Dead.* If it was true, if this wasn't a dream, and Maeve kept hoping it might be, then it meant she would never be anything else again but dead. Those she loved would talk about her in the past tense. They would think of her first as a grave and then as a person. Or maybe the body lying in the Museum Gardens would become ashes. She might have preferred that, since she had been scattered just the same in life. *You're all over the place,* her mum had said about her once. Now, she would be.

"Yes," Hel answered in that blunt, emotionless way. Her brows furrowed with what looked to be sympathy. "You're between life and death now, on a journey from one to the other. A little bit like an echo, there are pieces of your life still here, but they're difficult to reach."

So I am a ghost. Maeve supposed it made sense.

A gentle mew distracted her from her grief and she snapped her head to find Loki on the patchwork rug looking up at her. His eyes were narrowed to slits, hackles raised as they often were when the neighbor's dog walked past the window.

The sight of something familiar relieved Maeve and she lowered her hands to beckon to the cat. "Loki. Hello, Boy."

Hel sharpened, drawing her sceptre higher. "Why do you mention my father?"

Bewildered, Maeve frowned. It took her a moment for understanding to dawn on her. She'd read enough Norse mythology to remember that Loki — the god, not the cat — was named the father of the goddess of death, Hel.

The same Hel who claimed to be standing in front of her.

Then it was true: both the myths and Hel's claims. But if Maeve knew that, if she had that information stored, couldn't Hel be some sort of hallucination conjured by her near-death experience? Maybe she wasn't dead. Maybe she'd wake up in the hospital soon with no memory of any of this. Maybe this *was* just a dream.

How did one explain to a Norse goddess that Loki (the cat) had been named after a Marvel Cinematic Universe character based loosely on the same story? India was a Tom Hiddleston fan first and foremost, and that his character linked to Maeve's favorite mythology was only a happy coincidence.

"I was actually talking to the cat," she tried. "My roommate named him Loki."

Hel's attention fell to the poised tabby and she sunk into a crouch, leather armour creaking and stretching over thick long legs. "A cat," she repeated as though she'd never seen or heard of one before. "This creature is named after my father? They look nothing alike."

Maeve bit her bottom lip, the situation feeling slightly surreal. Particularly when Loki began to yowl in warning, his body arching further as though ready to pounce. Hel snarled back and he hissed before darting into the kitchen and disappearing through the cat flap.

"*Ha!*" Hel spat as though proud she had won this particular battle.

Maeve raised a brow. The goddess of death having it out with India's cat… Definitely a dream. A laugh bubbled inside her and she knew it was a result of fear rather than amusement. She tried to trap the rising panic, asking instead, "So if you're taking me to Hel… where is that? Is there some sort of portal or...?"

Rising to tower over Maeve again, Hel scoffed. "The gate to Helheim resides under a mountain in Ísland."

"Iceland?" Maeve repeated, only able to assume that's what Hel meant.

Hel nodded. "I am always able to find my way home, and yet..." She looked around. There was something so human about the disorientation on her face that, for a moment, Maeve forgot about the skeletal side of her. "I fear I've never been this far before."

"And you don't know how you got here?"

"I remember only darkness as I followed the call of the Norns." At Maeve's confusion, she explained, "The Fates. Which led me to you. One moment, I was riding away from Hekla. The next..." — she extended her arms — "here."

Hekla. Maeve knew that name. It had been in the news this morning. A volcanic eruption in Iceland, images of thick black soot rising from an angry mountain. Flights around Europe had been cancelled, locals evacuating their towns and villages.

"Hekla is erupting! In this world, at least. Could that have something to do with all this?" She'd watched enough *Doctor Who* to know that parallel universes could sometimes fold together, that rifts could poke a hole in the world with a single event. She'd never believed it to be real before now, mind, but neither had she thought gods and goddesses existed.

Hel contemplated, returning to the couch beside Maeve. It tilted like a seesaw, causing Maeve to grip the arm, alarmed.

"It seemed as though Hekla had been angered as I left the gates, too. Perhaps you're right, Skjaldmær. Perhaps the natural order of things has been disrupted."

That nickname again, as though Maeve not being a true

shield-maiden made no difference to Hel's perception of her.

She took a deep breath, wondering what that meant: both the grand title and the fact that the world seemed to have imploded. Would India and her family feel the effects, too, or was it only the souls Hel came to claim?

"If all of this is an accident, a mistake, where will I go?" she asked quietly, afraid to hear the answer. "I don't belong in your world but I can't stay here either, can I?" She certainly didn't want to, not if her only company was Loki the cat. It was too quiet. She wouldn't last a day without going mad.

Hel shook her head, jaw set in determination. From this angle, Maeve could only see the flesh part of her face, she looked almost human. Beautiful. Fierce. Her eyes were so dark they seemed to swallow the light, her nose aquiline and her lips full and red. Her cheekbones were high, brow thick enough to cast shadows. If either of them were a warrior, it was her. She was no traditional goddess, but Maeve could certainly imagine her raw power in war.

"The Norns don't make mistakes," Hel said. "If I found you, it was because I was meant to, skjaldmær or not." She turned to face Maeve, revealing that white, skeletal part. Maeve forced her gaze to remain unwavering and found it easier than expected. Where before, those features had terrified her, now, she was intrigued. Disarmed. Committed to understanding whatever dream or nightmare or afterlife this was. It wasn't often one got to look upon a goddess. Perhaps Maeve should make the most of it. After all, it was the only face she could see at the moment. Hel was the only person willing to guide her.

Their eyes met across the couch. Hel's seemed to wrap Maeve up like a security blanket. For just a moment, her fear and anguish ebbed. And then she caught sight of a photograph hanging on the wall. It showed India in her cap and gown, degree in hand. Maeve posed beside her wearing her prettiest dress, there to support her best friend's graduation day.

Maeve would never get another day like that. She'd never get another day with India, would never celebrate another milestone, hers or otherwise. She'd never fall in love again or settle down or buy her first house.

"I wasn't meant to die this young," she whispered, a tear rolling down her cheek as her heart was dragged down, down, down. "I was meant..."

She didn't know what she'd been meant for. If she had, she wouldn't have been living on her friend's couch. Still, at least she'd had the possibility of more then. Now there was nothing. Just a yawning expanse of unknown.

She shook her head, unwilling to feel sorry for herself for a moment longer. "I feel like none of this is real. Like maybe I'm dreaming." She shuffled closer to Hel without meaning to, trying to search for any sign that she'd conjured the goddess from her imagination. But no drawing or image or cosplay could have compared to the real woman, the way she seemed to command the air, making it cold as ice. The way the darkness clung to her like a lover unwilling to leave.

And Hel had touched her earlier. Maeve had felt so much in that touch. She wondered now what it would feel like to do the same; whether that might bring her some understanding.

Hel met Maeve's hand halfway across the couch and pressed it to her firm chest, covered in layers as it was. She felt no heartbeat, not one that she was used to, but something lived under that armour all the same. Something that hummed and flowed like a burbling stream. The only thing that still felt alive in this room.

"It's real," Hel said. "This is no dream."

When her hand dropped, Maeve didn't pull away, instead letting her fingers creep to that strange, uncovered part of Hel's face. "Could I?"

"You have never seen a face like this before." It wasn't a question. "Most dare not look at it, let alone touch it. Not at first, anyway."

Maeve took the statement as permission and gently ran a fingertip along the contours of bone and sinew. The skeleton was dry like old parchment, but still smooth. It was clear Hel still felt things there by the way she stiffened beneath Maeve, the way her lips parted.

"It's difficult *not* to look at it." Maeve pulled away, half-embarrassed, half-mesmerised. The goddess looked slightly less scary now. Almost trustworthy.

"Because it is ugly?"

"No." She could never describe something so unique, so elaborate, so impossible, to be ugly. "No, because it's stunning."

Curiosity brightened Hel's features but it was gone quickly as she stood. "We must go. I need to return to my people, make sure they're safe. Are you to join me, Skjaldmær?"

What other option did she have? There was no one else here, nobody to bring her back.

She nodded, feeling dizzy as she looked at the goddess's looming figure. Perhaps there was a little bit of Brunhild in her after all. "If the Norns will it, who am I to test fate?"

Hel's answering grin was wolfish and otherworldly — and, Maeve suspected, proud.

Chapter Five

Maeve had never ridden a horse before, and she had never guessed her first try would be on a strange three-legged mount ready to take her to the afterlife. She stood awkwardly as Hel waited for her to get on, looking up and down the street as though a neighbour might appear at any moment. But nobody came. Save for the rain pelting the shiny concrete, there was nothing here. It left Maeve soggy, and she asked, "Why can't I touch things, but the rain can touch me?"

Hel sighed, readjusting her steed's saddle. "So many questions."

"I know," Maeve retorted. "It's almost as though I've never died before."

"You mortals never were very funny." Hel patted her horse's back. "Come on. Up."

But she was so tall — had to be to support a giantess — and she couldn't forget the visible ribs, nor was she entirely sure where Hel wanted to take her. What was Hel, really? Maeve had never thought the afterlife was a physical place. Her interest in mythology and history had only extended to the basic things: Odin, Thor, the scrummy bearded Vikings on Netflix. "Where are we going? I mean, which direction?"

A raised eyebrow. "Helhest will know where to take us. She always knows the way."

"Oh, good," muttered Maeve. "Let's rely on a horse to get me to the afterlife." She hooked her foot into the stirrup, which required a flexibility she hadn't exercised since ballet classes at eight years old. Grabbing the black leather seat, she tried to hoist herself up with an "Oof!" — and failed miserably, stumbling down with her foot still stuck.

Two hands caught her before she hit the ground and pushed her up roughly. Her breath caught in her throat as she was slung through the air and then finally seated on Helhest's back. At least the horse was patient, although it did let out an amused snort at Maeve's incompetence.

Hel mounted behind her and then her thick thighs were bracketing Maeve's, arms encasing her torso as she grabbed the reins.

"Not so hard, was it?" Her voice was a low rumble in the shell of Maeve's ear, vibrating against Maeve from deep in her chest.

Strange, fuzzy warmth spread through Maeve like pins and needles. She hadn't been this close to anybody in a while, she certainly hadn't been this close to a goddess before. So close she could smell smoke and earth and leather curling around her with Hel's presence, reminding her of petrichor in the humid heat of summer. Her breath left her shakily. "Not for you, perhaps. Your horse is almost as big as a house."

"The rain can touch you because you're part of its nature, Skjaldmær, just as it is part of you. You cannot touch things from your old life, but that doesn't mean everything is unreachable. You haven't ceased existing. You just exist differently now."

Existing differently is better than not existing at all. She closed her eyes and steeled herself for whatever came next, something restless writhing inside of her. Perhaps she was more ready to move on than she thought. But something kept her tethered, drawing her focus back to the apartment.

"There's no way to say goodbye to my friends? My family?"

"You should have said your goodbyes before entering your battle,'" Hel replied.

As though Maeve could have known. With tears glistening in her eyes, she bid the house and India a silent goodbye and hoped that one day they would be reunited. She could only imagine the aftermath of her death and it made her ache to think that she'd never know why she was killed. Whether it had been pure accident, pure carelessness, or something more. Would the woman be arrested? Would there be support for her loved ones?

Will I be remembered at all?

"Okay," she whispered, wiping her damp cheeks. "I'm ready."

Hel's thigh nudged Maeve's and then they were galloping away from Moss Street, away from everything Maeve knew. She was glad for the body curled around hers, protecting her from the wind and rain, as lightning lit up the gloomy sky and the storm raged on.

*   *   *

Hel recognized York for what it was when she reached the battlefield a second time that day. The echoes of old invasions flickered like smoke around her as she helped Maeve off Hester before doing the same.

"Jorvik," she said aloud. "I took many warriors from this place. I didn't recognize it before, but... of course."

Maeve glanced at her as though surprised, sadness gleaming

in her eyes as she looked upon the place where she had died. Her braids whispered in the wind, falling free of their restraints so that silver strands whipped across her face.

"I can't imagine how much you must have seen," she said. "How many cities and battles. How much blood and death. Doesn't it ever get to be too much?"

"Blood and death is my calling." A poor attempt at evading the question, because she was afraid that one day the answer might be yes. She hadn't chosen this life, not really. It had been Odin's way of casting her out, her fate decided for her not by Norns but by him and his coldness. She didn't know who she would be otherwise, and there was no use imagining. Blood was her life. Death was her life. It surrounded her in everything she did. It was her home, just as Helheim was. Maeve wandered further into the battlefield, where debris still littered the trodden grass and there, blood where she had fallen to take her last breath.

"My body isn't here anymore," Maeve said.

"It would have been taken by now. In my world, buried, burned, or sent to sea."

"It's not too different here." She crossed her arms over her chest. "Although it'll probably be kept in a morgue. That's strange to think about." Maeve shivered and something tugged in Hel's stomach. An urge to step forward, get closer, reach out.

Instead, she returned to Helhest, running her fingers through her midnight mane as she observed the foul weather. The storm only proved something was awry, the howling wind reminding her of battle cries.

"We should continue on. It's clear there's nothing here." Usually, the rift back to Gjallarbrú opened close to the battle, to the body, taking the warrior to be judged by Modgud before they passed the river Gjöll. It had never taken this long to get home before, and Helhest was too still, as though she didn't know the way. Hel didn't know whether to blame Maeve's dramatics earlier or see it for what it was: another sign that something was wrong. "How far are we from Hekla?"

Maeve's eyes widened. "I wasn't much good at geography but I'm pretty sure we're an ocean away."

Then they would need a boat. A sturdy one, if this storm was to continue and the rift was to remain closed. A foreign anxiety tingled across her skin but she clenched her jaw, refusing to show it as she climbed back onto her mount. "Let's go."

"Where?" asked Maeve. "How?" She brushed her hair out of her eyes, rain spitting down her face. "This isn't... None of this is right."

"This again," Hel grumbled. As sympathetic and confused as she was, she was tired of having to convince a mortal to come with her. If this woman was not a skjaldmær, what made her so worthy of this much trouble? If the Norns would will it, she would abandon her and wipe all of this from her mind, but it seemed this crumbling world had other ideas.

"Yes, this again!" Maeve erupted. "I'm scared. I'm not ready to leave behind everything I know. This isn't right!"

"It is not my duty to comfort you, Skjaldmær!" Hel boomed over the thunder, her eyelashes dripping rainwater and her voice dripping venom. "It is my duty to lead you to the afterlife and you are making it incredibly difficult!" She fisted her hand around the sceptre and jabbed the air with it. "You should be honored I have come for you but you hardly seem worthy of the honor. Would you prefer to remain here, allow your spirit to dwindle less and less until one day you are simply gone? Or would you like to stop wasting my time and help me to get back

35

to Hekla so we can both put this to rest?"

Maeve's throat bobbed, her face crumpling. She sank to her knees without warning, covering her mouth as though trying to cram her sobs back down her throat.

Hel pursed her lips in a thin, impatient line, waiting for her to put herself back together. Waiting for the shield-maiden in her to reveal itself.

But it didn't. The woman's pain kept pouring out of her until she was gripping fistfuls of ruined grass and mud, her face paint running down her cheeks in black streaks. "This isn't right," she said again and again. "This isn't real. Please, wake up, Maeve. Please."

Hel had never seen anything like it. Such devastation in one small person. She dismounted Helhest and slowly traipsed back toward Maeve, unsure if she wanted to shake her into action or hold her so that she wouldn't fall apart completely and wipe herself from this world. Her own chin wobbled with uncertainty as she found a middle ground, placing her hand on Maeve's shuddering shoulder.

Gradually, the sobs ebbed. The rain rolled down Maeve's hunched back, her teeth chattering as she bowed her head to the earth. They stayed that way for a long time, through violent peals of thunder, neither of them moving. Just when Hel was certain she would have to drag the woman onto Hester herself, just when she was certain she was a lost cause, Maeve rose on shaky legs. Without looking at Hel, she walked back to the horse.

Hel followed, waiting until Maeve had hooked her heel in the stirrup to boost her onto the saddle, this time gently with her hands around the woman's soft hips. Without a word, Hel mounted and grabbed the reins — and as Helhest began to walk in a new direction, Maeve sunk into Hel's torso as though she no longer had the energy to hold herself up.

Despite Hel's better judgment, she let her.

Chapter Six

"If you are no shield-maiden and there were no battles to fight, what was it you did in this odd realm?"

The question drew Maeve from her trance. She'd been lost in her own exhaustion as the horse carried them toward Hull, where Maeve had told Hel the nearest port was. It seemed that Helhest hadn't needed directing anyhow. Hel had barely needed to lift the reins as they raced through the night, following by the side of a dead motorway.

The world had never been so quiet — at least, between the storm's scarce intervals — and yet in Maeve's head, it was so loud. She kept waiting to feel at peace with her death. Kept wondering when she would stop thinking of her body in the gardens.

"I was…" She only realised after she began talking that there was nothing she could say. She hadn't found out what she was yet, and now it was too late. "I was unemployed, actually."

"Like most of the gods," Hel muttered, bitterness dripping into her tone. Buildings began to appear, nothing more than square silhouettes, but already, Maeve could taste the salty sea air. "What of your family?"

"My mum and dad…" She didn't want to think of her parents. She hadn't seen them since her visit home last Christmas, and now she couldn't even remember the last conversation she'd had with her mum. Probably an argument about cheating at Monopoly. She was a sensitive, introverted woman who Maeve had never completely understood, where Dad had always been the one cracking jokes and checking in on her. She wasn't sure how they'd take Maeve's death, and for the first time, was glad she couldn't find out. "They lived an hour or two away, so we haven't seen each other in a while. Other than that, it's just me. And my best friend, India."

"No partner?" Hel's body shifted against Maeve's. She felt warm where Maeve was cold. She wondered how they would have looked in the normal world. A giantess and a woman wearing a costume. A Norse goddess and a nobody.

Maeve frowned, wondering why Hel was the one prodding now where before she hadn't wanted to talk. "What was it you said? 'So many questions'?"

"I have never met somebody like you before." Hel's voice was closer now, her breath tickling Maeve's ear. "Forgive me for being curious."

"Forgive me for being boring," Maeve retorted. "No, no partner."

Cranes rose in front of them as they passed through a roundabout. A moment later, Maeve glimpsed the moonlight rippling off the black sea and couldn't help but shrink. The waves were beastly and the industrial lots surrounding her were a stark reminder that she was no longer in York, no longer surrounded by history and beauty.

Was Hel really going to take her to Iceland? Could they even *get* to Iceland? Maeve certainly couldn't captain a boat and she doubted a Norse goddess knew much about modern ships.

"Boring is not the word I'd use. Irksome, maybe. Peculiar,

perhaps. Not boring."

Maeve huffed. It was clear that Hel understood nothing of "mortals," as she called them, especially ones in the process of grieving their own life. It occurred to her then that, if they really were headed to the gates of Hel, Maeve would never see her own world again. She'd be somewhere new, somewhere terrifying. Who would keep her company? She doubted the goddess herself would have time to help Maeve settle in.

Brows furrowing, she asked, "What is Hel like? Because we're told it's all fire and brimstone for those who don't belong in Heaven."

"I don't see what is wrong with fire and brimstone." Maeve felt Hel shrug against her and whipped her head around fearfully only to find the corner of Hel's mouth quirking with the beginnings of a grin. A joke. She was joking.

"Niflheim is the place people do not wish to end up. It is a land of ice and mist. But Helheim... that is home. A land of peace. It is where life continues. Gardens and forests grow and my people often hold celebrations in the streets. The seasons come to visit and the stars sparkle at night. It can be cold and bleak like any other realm, but it can also be a place worth living. It could be *your* place. Will be, given we make it back to Hekla."

Maeve couldn't quite picture a place so far away yet so similar to the world she knew. The words gave her some comfort, yes, but they gave her no better understanding of where she was going. "And what would I do there? How would I spend my time?"

"Well, we need somebody to slay the ice trolls."

Maeve choked on her own breath. "What?"

Hel's low, smoky chuckle rocked through them both, an

40

unexpectedly tender sound that made Maeve want to join in.

Instead, she sighed. "You're joking. Again."

"Yes, I jest, Skjaldmær. You are free to choose how you live in my kingdom. Some prefer to keep busy with farming or running businesses, just as they did in their past lives. Others prefer to keep to themselves after a long time spent in battle. Some volunteer as guards or fighters. There will always be unrest among the realms, though I try to keep Helheim out of it these days."

Worrying at her lip, Maeve responded, "What if I don't fit in there? I never figured out what I wanted to do here. What if I don't..." *Belong*, she almost said, but she stifled that word quickly, thinking it silly.

Only it was true. She wasn't particularly good at anything. She certainly didn't wish to live on a farm among strangers, nor did she want to spend her afterlife isolated and bored. She wouldn't even think about the latter, the "unrest." *Better not to know.*

"There must be something that would bring you joy?" Hel said, confusion shimmering in her tone. She pulled at the reins and Hester turned the next corner, bringing them closer to the docks.

There was nothing blocking the view of the vast ocean now. Nothing standing between Maeve and the unknown. Her stomach twisted.

"The reenactments brought me joy. Pretending to be a warrior," she admitted, looking down at her cold, red hands. "Look how well that turned out."

"The good news is that you cannot die twice." Hel hopped off the horse without warning, her boots thudding on the concrete. She squinted, her face dappled by rain as she looked toward

41

the edge of the dock.

A shadow loomed there. It took a moment to take shape. Maeve was certain it was some sort of ship.

"Is that...?" Hel muttered under her breath, stepping closer. Her attention snapped back to Maeve and she held out a hand. This time, it was the skeletal one, all gray and knobbly and strange. "Come on."

Maeve deliberated, wary to accept something that should have been grotesque, horrific. But she'd already run her fingers along Hel's face and Hel had not harmed her.

Her fingers curled around Hel's bony palm as she jumped down. Surprisingly, it did not feel strange. In fact, it was warm compared to Maeve's skin, which felt frostbitten and numb. She pulled away to wrap her arms around her torso, teeth chattering in the wind as, together, they walked toward the ship, Helhest following closely.

It was like no ferry Maeve had ever seen before. It was something she had only ever found pictured in history books and on the television before now: a longship. Only, the wood was a strange yellowing color and it was far bulkier, as though it had been merged with a pirate ship. At the prow, a serpent's head had been carved, and though it was impossible, the wood seemed to shimmer as though covered in black scales.

"Holy shit," Maeve whispered, craning her neck.

For the first time, she wondered if perhaps all of this was real.

"I don't know what that means," Hel said, "but I agree."

42

Chapter Seven

Hel had never been more elated to see *Naglfar*. The longship towered like a god above the dock, casting she and Maeve in its vast, menacing shadow. This ship represented all that she despised: long journeys, war. But now it was the only thing that kept her from losing her grip in this strange new reality. She might have sunk to her knees were it not for her dignity. As it was, she squared her shoulders, clasping her sceptre tightly as she thanked the gods for those billowing sails.

The tall, brawny figure of the jötunn captain cut through the waning moonlight at the ship's prow and Hel felt Maeve stumble back in surprise at her side. But Hel could only grin at the fire giant. "Hrym, you old dog!" she bellowed into the wind, cupping her hand over her mouth to be better heard over the storm.

Something between a growl and a throaty laugh was her response as Hrym stepped forward, peering at them from above. "Well, well, well. What have we here?" His grin was wolfish and half-hidden behind his scruffy red beard. "Is that a goddess I spot?"

"How did you find us?" Hel asked, relief washing through her — relief she hadn't known she needed until now.

"*Naglfar* always takes me where I'm needed." He patted the railings of the boat with familiar adoration and Hel rolled her eyes.

"Sentimental old troll."

Maeve sputtered as though the storm had blown something foul into her mouth. "*Troll?*"

Before Hel could respond, Hrym continued, "And who may the mortal be? An exciting new addition to that godsforsaken kingdom of yours?"

Though she knew it was said in jest, Hel still bristled. She was quite tired of defending Helheim, especially from her own people. Though she ruled over the underworld and was the daughter of Loki, her mother had been jötunn as Hrym was, and she had grown up in the land of the giants until she was cast down by Odin. Immortal beings, jötnar rarely had use for an afterlife, and many of her own believed Hel's duty to be redundant. She knew that they must laugh at her, must think her stupid, and she was quite content to let them — behind her back.

If they dared say it in front of her... well, she wouldn't be quite so polite.

As though sensing it, Hrym straightened and cleared his throat. "Why don't you come aboard? You're a long way from home, dear Hel. A long way indeed."

"You'll get us back to Hekla." It wasn't a question and she made sure to keep her voice sharp with authority. She resisted the urge to glance at Maeve to gauge her response, though the woman's shivering fear radiated in waves.

Not just fear. Hel had only felt that coldness a few times before and her stomach had clenched the moment she'd sensed it on Maeve. She was cold, freezing even — because she was dwindling. Her spirit needed to settle somewhere, find its destination, and without Hel's usual ways of bringing her warriors home, it was taking too long.

Her soul was lost. If it was not found soon... it might be too late.

"We're not going with him, are we?" Maeve whispered.

"He's our only way home," Hel replied, her brows furrowing. *He's your only chance at an afterlife*, she wanted to say, but she didn't wish to frighten the woman even more. She'd been through enough today and, besides, Hel couldn't know for certain. She'd never witnessed a soul give in firsthand. Would never stick around long enough. She'd only heard of those who refused to pass on to another realm disappearing altogether, their soul lost to the void. To nothing.

Hel clenched her fist. She wouldn't let that happen. Not now, and certainly not to Maeve.

At the sight of Maeve's trepidation, she softened and, without thinking, curled her hand around Maeve's wrist. Her skin was icy, her arm so narrow Hel could loop her entire hand around it and then some. Maeve looked down as though surprised by Hel's touch — but she didn't seem unhappy with it, nor afraid.

"We can trust him, Skjaldmær. Can you trust me?"

She felt Hrym's watchful gaze on them, but he said nothing as Maeve deliberated. Finally, she nodded her head.

"Good." Hel offered her a reassuring smile — as reassuring as she could muster, at least, for somebody who had never much cared for consoling people before. It must have worked, because Maeve attempted a weary smile back.

Looking up, Hel shouted, "We're coming aboard!"

A moment later, Hrym let down the ramp. Hel motioned for Maeve to go first, but as she stepped onto the walkway, a vicious wave curled over them, threatening to wash them away. Hel grabbed Maeve quickly, pulling her back with a rough, fumbling grip that stole a gasp from the very pits of Maeve's chest.

"Careful," Hel whispered, glaring at the sea as though she could tame the waves with a look. Unfortunately, the sea was defiant tonight, spurred by the gusting winds the way Hester was spurred by the Norns' call.

"What was it you said? I can't die twice?"

"No, but I wouldn't recommend testing it. You can still drown as anyone else can, and I've heard that isn't pleasant — even without the dying part."

"That doesn't seem fair," Maeve murmured, and only as she craned her neck did Hel realize how close they were. She could feel Maeve's body brushing against hers with each breath, that strange silvery hair curling into Hel's face. She smelled like sweat and roses after rain.

As her heart began to pound, Hel pulled away, making sure to maintain a steady grip on Maeve as she aided her aboard. Maeve's boots slipped once more against the wet bone of the ramp, and then they were on the ship, with her gripping onto one of the poles for dear life. She looked up at it, a line burrowing between her brows as she took in the fingernails forged with bones. Pulling away slowly and wiping her palm on her trousers, she stuttered out, "Erm... those aren't real, are they?"

Hrym laughed from the quarterdeck. "Where on Midgard did you find this odd one?"

"For my own sanity, I'll take that as a no," she murmured.

Hel only grimaced. Perhaps it was better Maeve didn't know how this ship had come to be and what it was made of —

fingernails and bones of the dead. Were they not so far from Jorvik now, Maeve's physical body might have contributed to some maintenance. That wasn't a thought Hel particularly enjoyed, though she didn't know why. It was an honor for warriors to continue their lives both in the spiritual and physical sense: their souls found peace and their remains continued journeying through the seas and fjords with *Naglfar*. Yet the thought of those fingernails and bones belonging to the crumpled body she'd seen on the battlefield in Jorvik....

She couldn't think of it. Didn't have to as she went halfway down the ramp to guide up Helhest. "Come on, Hester," she murmured. "Time to go home."

She hoped that's where they were going, at least.

* * *

Maeve trembled as she looked up at the craggy-faced giant. He was painted with the scars and tattoos of black runes not unlike the ones she'd seen imitated on the skin of Viking reenactors once or twice.

But that's all they'd been. Imitations. This man was no imitation.

He was just as tall as Hel and twice as terrifying. His beard fell to his stomach, wind-tousled hair just as long and knotted behind his shoulders. His armor shone an unnatural bronze as though hit by the sun, though nothing but the gloom embraced them. The boat seemed to ripple when he moved, or perhaps that was the waves.

And the ship...

The ship made her nauseous. She was quite certain the fingernails were real, quite certain that she was on the legendary

Naglfar. The crew was made of seated giants rowing their oars, lit by an eerie yellow light glowing from inner cabins beneath the quarterdeck. Maeve gulped and held onto the railings despite her better judgement, the wind tearing through the sails with a vicious bite.

"What do you know of this trouble with the realms?" Hel's voice cut sharply through the rain as she made to stand beside Hrym.

"I know unrest wracks through the world along with these godsforsaken waves," Hrym murmured. "I was carrying warriors across the sea when the tempest brought me here. I assumed for good reason." He glanced at Maeve over his shoulder, his eyes the colour of fire. "That one's a funny-looking thing. Is she quite well?"

Hel set her exposed jaw, the visible tendons twitching like snakes writhing around her bones. "She isn't like the others. She comes from another world. A strange world where there are felines bearing my father's name."

Hrym let out a booming guffaw. "Ha! He would certainly love that! It would do wonders for his ego."

Hel smirked.

Perplexed and on the edge of it all, Maeve wiped her cheeks with her sleeves, feeling soaked to the bone and already tired of rocking with the ship. Her skin didn't feel like her own anymore and she imagined herself drifting for moments at a time like her feet were no longer touching the ground.

She felt like a real ghost.

"Then she is no shield-maiden?" the captain asked, fingers curling around the oar. Like the rest of the ship and Hel's sceptre, the spokes and wheel were made of bones and she couldn't look for too long.

"Perhaps not," said Hel, "but the Norns still wanted me to find her."

"Or she means nothing at all, because the world is imploding and we're all destined to die, Norns or no," Hrym suggested. "Has Ragnarök finally come?"

Hel's features seemed to shutter as though she refused to entertain the idea. Even so, Maeve hadn't missed the flicker that had come before. Fear. For the first time, she had witnessed Hel looking fearful.

It made her shudder, too.

"Ragnarök shall never come," Hel answered in a low, threatening voice. "She means *something*."

He glanced at Maeve again, disgust colouring his features. "She looks as though a strong breeze might take her out. Better we throw her overboard now and save ourselves the hassle—"

It happened all at once. Hel swiped her feet beneath Hrym and he fell to the floor with an almighty thwack, leaving the deck to splinter beneath him. Maeve hopped away, alarmed, as Hel drove her sceptre against his neck with a nasty snarl. Rain dripped from her face as though desperate to get away and the crew of slightly less-imposing giants below stopped to stare at the spectacle.

"You may be the captain of this ship, troll, but I am the goddess of death," Hel spat. "I could wipe you from all the realms in one moment if I wanted to. I could kill you and make your afterlife a waking nightmare. I have been known to do far worse. So, if I were you, I'd keep your mouth fastened shut when it comes to the girl. You will not harm her. You will not even look at her unless I will it. Am I quite clear?"

Gormless, Maeve's hand rose to her mouth, terror ringing through her. This was not the woman who'd promised her safety. This was something else, a chillingly lethal monster.

A monster who is protecting me, Maeve realized. A monster who had never raised a weapon against Maeve. Who had watched her cry as her world ended with her hand on Maeve's shoulder.

"Hel…" Maeve whispered it, unsure what else there was to say. She only knew that she had to say *something*.

The thunder boomed louder than ever as Hel's head whipped up, her one black eye finding Maeve. Her upper lip was still curled, spittle flying from her teeth, and Maeve's gaze turned pleading. She stepped back, unable to hide her fear.

"Who is she, this girl?" croaked Hrym.

Hel didn't reply, her bottomless gaze still fixed on Maeve. Slowly, she released Hrym from the sceptre's grip and straightened.

"Nobody," she said, but her voice shook as she turned on her heel. "She is nobody. But she is mine, Hrym, and I decide what happens to her. She will remain unharmed. She belongs in Helheim."

"I have no intention of hurting her, dear Hel," Hrym said, holding his arms up in surrender. "No need for theatrics." Unlike Hel, no sign of death clung to him. He was all flesh, minus a strange, rocky band around his wrist that glowed like hot coals. Maeve was too distracted to figure out if it was some accessory or another bizarre giant thing.

She breathed a sigh of relief as Hel gave Hrym space, landing just in front of Maeve. She sniffed. "I'm glad to hear it. Now, is there somewhere we can rest for a moment?"

He nodded, clumsily rising to his feet and resuming his hold on the oar. "Use the captain's quarters as your own. It seems I won't have time to take my hand from the wheel in such a storm."

With a nod, Hel spun on her heel and motioned for Maeve to follow. Her face was filled with shadows, back quickly turned as they descended the steps. The stares of the gigantic crew followed them all the way into the captain's cabin.

Chapter Eight

Hel ground her teeth together as she yanked off her long cape and threw it over a chair. Her bones still shook with a fury she wasn't used to having to control. She'd been alone too long, distancing herself from all but those she trusted to help run her kingdom. That, and not many tried to threaten her or her people.

And when they did, she didn't often care quite so much.

She pinched her forehead before looking at Maeve, who stood motionless before the door. She was lit by the glow of Hrym's hearth, a blessing that could only be found on the ship of a fire giant. Her teeth clattered together, body trembling.

Hel tutted, moving to help her out of her damp clothes — but Maeve flinched and Hel halted.

Afraid. She is afraid of me.

She'd seen it on the quarterdeck too, when Hel had pinned Hrym down. Hel's vision had blurred, her entire being made of fire and ice and the storm above as she thought of the captain throwing Maeve overboard. She knew the jötnar's attitude toward mortals. Knew Hrym wouldn't think twice if he thought it might aid them. Hel couldn't let that happen. For whatever reason, Maeve was fated to join her in the underworld.

Stepping backward to give her space, Hel whispered, "I will not hurt you, Skjaldmær. You need not be afraid."

Maeve's lips pursed into a thin line as she looked anywhere but at Hel. "What happens now? How long will we be on this ship?" Maeve's hand drifted to her stomach. "I was seasick when I was alive. I don't particularly enjoy being rocked about."

"*Naglfar* travels faster than most," Hel said, using a splint and the fire to light a lantern. She placed it on the captain's desk, muscles stiff as she attempted not to sway with the choppy waves. "It shouldn't take us more than two days or so."

Cautiously, Maeve sat cross-legged by the hearth, reaching out her rain-reddened fingers. Her skin glowed golden, so full of colour that Hel forgot for a moment she was no longer alive. A bright, frightened soul lingering between life and death.

Unease caused Hel's stomach to clench. She didn't dare try to come near Maeve again. "I would find you some warmer clothes, but something tells me Hrym would not have anything that would fit you." She sniffed, searching the cabin again. Armour and weapons hung from the walls — and there, draped on a hook, a tatty old cape. She pulled it down and walked slowly toward Maeve, wary of doing anything that might make her cower again. It made Hel conscious of her own size for the first time in her life. Made her conscious that, to a mortal like Maeve, Hel might be considered more than just jötnar. She might be considered monstrous.

"Here," Hel offered.

Maeve paused before tentatively taking the cape.

"You should take off your clothes," Hel advised.

"Excuse me?" Maeve snapped.

Hel raised her brows innocently, though she found her focus drifting down Maeve's frame, wondering what it was about

53

those curves that might make her so chaste. "To warm up. It is no good staying in damp clothes. If you take them off, they will dry quicker."

"Oh." Maeve paused, seeming to consider the fire, then the cape. "All right. Then... turn around."

Hel grunted but did as she was told. "Mortals are so strange when it comes to modesty."

Shuffling ensued, Maeve's footsteps stumbling over each other as she undressed. She made it sound like a difficulty, huffs and puffs escaping her. "Do goddesses prefer to walk around nude?"

Hel shrugged. "Sometimes. I certainly do not fear others seeing my body." Or she hadn't, until Maeve had looked at her for the first time, eyes round with fear as she took in the left side of her face, the part that resembled a corpse.

"How is it that I can take off my clothes as I would any other day but I couldn't touch anything in my own house earlier?"

"I told you," she said, "your soul is between life and death. You can only interact with things that are part of your transition. Your clothes can be taken with you, but the house... you are not supposed to be part of that world anymore."

"So I'm a ghost."

"I suppose you would be if you were staying on Midgard, yes. If that's how you see it."

The room turned cold and Hel fought the urge to turn around; make sure Maeve wasn't due another one of her dramatic episodes. She couldn't handle many more of those. But she heard no sniveling, and when Maeve permitted it, Hel found her engulfed in the cape like it was a blanket, her clothes drying on the rug beside her. She sat back down, seeming to fall into a trance as she watched the flames dance in the hearth.

54

Restless, Hel began to search Hrym's cabin again, this time for something better than a dusty old cape. If they were going to do this, Hel needed something strong.

She browsed cupboards and drawers to find a painted barrel, pulled out the stopper and sniffed. Fermented barley and bitter juniper overwhelmed her senses and she thanked the Norns for her good fortune. Thankfully, Hrym already had a wooden cup on his desk, still stained by his last drink. She poured the beer into it before taking a swig. The strong spice warmed her throat.

"Here," she said, offering the drink down to Maeve.

She took it with reluctance, holding her nose to the rim of the cup before grimacing. "What is it?"

"Beer. A nice strong brew. It'll take the edge off — and the cold." Hel hoped, at least. She wasn't so sure the cold would be easy to chase away, not as long as they were so far from the gates, the underworld. Her resting place.

Maeve took a large gulp, her mouth contorting with distaste. But still, she went back in for another glug before handing the cup back. "I'm glad there's still alcohol in the afterlife. I could murder a mojito."

Hel frowned at the foreign word. "A *what?*"

"It's a cocktail with white rum, mint, and lime. Much more refreshing than whatever is in there."

Though she wasn't sure she understood, Hel nodded all the same. How different they were. She found herself so curious about the life Maeve led before all of this.

She didn't realise she was staring until Maeve met her eyes, shadows dappling her features as the flames guttered. Her eyes were near silver in the dim light and Hel couldn't help but be drawn to the pale column of her bare neck, the shifting collar bones as she adjusted the cloak around her.

"So Hrym and his crew... they're trolls?" Maeve asked, shivering slightly.

"Jötnar. Giants."

"And you're one, too?

Hel passed the cup back to Maeve, shifting on her feet. *Should I sit? Remain standing?* There was so much distance between them this way, she had to look down her crooked nose to see Maeve.

She gave in, lowering herself to the floor as gracefully as somebody of her build could, pulling one foot in and bending the opposite knee to balance her elbow on. Maeve didn't shuffle away, didn't appear scared anymore, her lips pink from the beer and a faraway look in her eyes.

"I'm many things, but yes. I was born in Jotunheim, as was my mother," she said softly.

"And Loki, the trickster god... he's your father?"

Her lips curled sourly. "Yes."

"How did you become the ruler of Hel? I mean..." — Maeve squeezed her eyes closed as though overwhelmed, shaking her head quickly — "you must have come first, to have the place named after you."

"Both me and my kingdom have been around for a very long time." Hel narrowed her gaze, looking into the fire and seeing her own land before she'd made it better. It had been much like Muspelheim, many demons and fire giants populating the land. She'd fought to send them away for eons before her warriors began arriving. "But yes. The underworld existed. It was me who branded it 'Helheim' once Odin cast me down. That is why my face looks the way it does. One doesn't survive the fall without a few scars."

"Why... why would he do that to you?"

An acidic taste sat on Hel's tongue as she thought of the god who had banished her. "He thought me dangerous. Claimed I asked too many questions about the gods and Valhalla. He was a paranoid old man who threw me from the skies out of fear I might challenge his position."

"And you were never allowed back?" Maeve whispered.

Hel shook her head, running her tongue along her teeth as she thought of the darkness she'd felt. The sense that her fall might never end, that she would always be suspended between realms. "I never wished to go back. Not if that's how they wished to treat me."

"So what happened after? How did Helheim come to be?"

"I crowned myself my own ruler. Made a place for those who were deemed unworthy of Valhalla but still deserved a meaningful afterlife." She inspected the dirt embedded in her fingernails as though the confession meant nothing. The truth of it was few people had ever asked about her life before she'd become a goddess. Few people cared, so long as she continued to stitch together the lines between life and death, forging a path, a future, for those who might not otherwise have had one.

She noticed Maeve's throat bob and narrowed her gaze, wondering what she was thinking. Wondering if she was still afraid.

"It sounds so lonely," Maeve breathed, voice soft with a tenderness Hel had never been offered before. From anyone.

Hel's breathing stuttered in surprise, something peculiar clogging her throat like clay. *It is lonely*, she realized only now. It had always been so lonely, and yet she'd been so driven by rage and spite that she hadn't cared. Even when she was surrounded by her kingdom, she had nobody.

The fact that Maeve had understood that, before even Hel could, made her feel vulnerable, like the remaining flesh had been peeled away and she was all bone, all skeleton now. Insides there for everyone to see. She snapped her head away, snatching the flask and downing the beer before wiping her mouth with her hand.

"I'm sorry," Maeve said. "I'm sorry you were treated that way."

And then a dainty hand was on Hel's knee. Hel blinked, puzzled. When was the last time somebody had touched her?

She knew she should have brushed Maeve away. Better to keep their boundaries simple and clear. But she couldn't bear to rid herself of this short, unexpected reprieve in the storm. The way Maeve had pushed aside her fear to trust Hel, to listen, to understand.

To see her as she was.

Hel put down the cup and covered Maeve's hand with her own. Her skin stung like ice and Hel hissed.

"You're freezing, Skjaldmær!" *Too* freezing. Hel's heart beat rapidly as she pressed the back of her hand to Maeve's forehead and Maeve's eyes fluttered shut. Hel had waded through icy rivers that were warmer than her.

"Can't seem to warm up," Maeve muttered, voice still gentle. She didn't know. Didn't understand what this meant.

Hel didn't dare tell her — because she refused to let it happen. She would get Maeve to Helheim, to home, and there she would live on. Warm. Free. Alive.

She refused to have it any other way, refused to let this woman the Norns had put on her path disappear.

Fruitlessly, Hel sidled closer and tightened the cloak around Maeve's shoulders, trying not to think of her naked body beneath. What it might look like. What it might feel like.

"There," she whispered, accidentally brushing Maeve's cheek with a skeletal finger. When Maeve only parted her lips as though surprised, her breath feathering across Hel, Hel stilled, lingering.

"I took it for granted," Maeve mumbled. "Being touched. Being able to feel things. I took all of it for granted when I was alive."

Touch me again, is what she seemed to be asking beneath those words. Hel prayed Maeve couldn't hear the thunder in her chest as she stroked Maeve's cheek again, this time dipping down to her chin. Her lips. They were like silk, plump and pink as berries. Beautiful. All of her beautiful and strange and otherworldly. A mortal who did not act or look mortal at all.

Did not feel mortal, either.

Hel journeyed across the other side of her face, across the peaks of her round cheeks and the line where skin met silver hair. Maeve bowed her head, leaning against Hel as though she couldn't hold herself up a moment longer.

"You must be tired," Hel murmured, though she didn't wish to pull away now. Didn't wish to ever stop tracing the lines of Maeve and her uncharted map. "You should get some rest."

Perhaps that would keep her spirit here, steady, for a little while longer. It had been a long day, and they had at least a few more to come. It couldn't have been easy for her.

With a faint nod, Maeve drew away and unfolded her legs. Hel grabbed a cushion from the nearest seat, stuffed with owl feathers and thrice the size of Maeve's head. She set it down beside her hips, motioning for Maeve to use it as she pleased. Slowly, Maeve brushed her hair off her shoulders and lowered to the floor, resting her head on the cushion. Her eyes fell shut instantly. Gently, Hel wiped a smudge of dirt from Maeve's nose. Maeve's lashes fluttered, breathing softening.

Asleep. Beside Hel, Maeve had fallen asleep.

Chapter Nine

"Are you going to tell me what makes that girl of yours so special?" Hrym asked, sniffing indifferently as Hel thudded up to the quarterdeck. It was clear he had taken Hel's aggression personally, but she did not have time to care about the captain's feelings.

The sea was more ferocious than it had been when they'd boarded, the crew scuttling across the deck as they tried to keep the ship upright and homebound. The worst storm Hel had ever had the displeasure of being caught in, and it was only getting worse.

If she was honest with herself, which she rarely was, she was afraid. Afraid of what awaited her at the foot of Hekla and afraid for Maeve. She'd been shivering in her sleep earlier, and when Hel had pressed the back of her hand to her forehead, it had been icier than the peak of Ísland's highest mountain. She hadn't wanted to leave her in the cabin alone, but after covering her with her own dried cape and a knitted throw for good measure, she knew she needed to gauge how long they had before Maeve's spirit faded completely.

She ground her jaw now, glaring into the swirling, choppy waves threatening to overthrow them all. "I never claimed she was special."

"You turned on one of your own to protect her," Hrym grumbled, his knuckles white around the spokes of the oar. The rain beat against his craggy face, his rusty hair and beard dark and drenched until the lightning lit the world an eerie shade of blue. "I'd like to believe you wouldn't do that for just any mortal. Otherwise, we are not the friends I believed us to be."

Sighing, Hel turned to face him, clutching the railing for support. She could keep lying if she wanted; let everybody believe she didn't care for Maeve, didn't worry for her. Or she could admit the truth: that she was fascinated by the skjaldmær and the way she seemed to feel so much. That she wanted Maeve to join Hel's kingdom not just because the Norns willed it, but because their story would feel unfinished otherwise. That when Hel had spoken of her past, her banishment, Maeve hadn't looked at her as though she was the goddess of death, a brutal warrior twice her size, but an equal. She'd spoken gently, offered understanding even though Hel's world was one Maeve would never belong to. And she'd done it willingly. Hel hadn't expected it, hadn't asked.

Maeve had seen, listened, empathized, all the same. She might not have been a warrior, but her heart bled right through that faux armour of hers and Hel had never seen that sort of unapologetic, unbridled strength before. Vulnerability, she'd learned, was a weapon in itself. One that struck Hel again and again until she was certain she'd fall to her knees.

"It's my job to keep her safe," Hel said finally, vying for some sort of middle ground. "The Norns brought me to her for a reason. You should respect that, Hrym. Stop questioning me."

Hrym gave her a flat, knowing look. "I have known you for too long to believe that's all it is. You have never been much good at hiding your heart, dear Hel."

"I don't know what you mean," she lied, her tone lowering with a warning.

He only shrugged, a smirk crossing his features. The fire glowing within him, through the rocks encasing his wrist, lit up the dark just slightly, causing his eyes to glint as he steered the ship.

Hel glared, but she still couldn't hide her worry. "How long until we reach land, do you think?"

"A day, perhaps, if we aren't all drowned before then. This storm…" — he glanced up at the sky with a weary expression — "I've never known anything like it. Not even the god of thunder could bring such a tempest. What if it really is the end for us?"

"It isn't!" Hel snapped. But she had no explanation for what was happening. Had it been Maeve's doing, somehow? Or was it the eruption she'd talked about, causing some sort of collapse among realms? The ground had been shaky as she'd crossed Gjallarbrú, before she'd passed into Jorvik and found Maeve.

If it was the latter, if the worlds were splitting apart and folding in on each other… what did that mean? Could it be fixed?

"I hope you're right," Hrym murmured, but his doubt was clear. That alone made Hel's heart beat faster. "Either way, there doesn't seem to be much hope for the mortal. Her spirit is dwindling. We all feel it here. She may not last the voyage."

A sharp spike lanced through Hel and she straightened with renewed anger, though she had already been thinking the same. But for him to say it as though it didn't matter, as though *Maeve* didn't matter….

"That's why you will get us there quickly!" she spat.

"I cannot control these waves—"

63

"You will do it!" Hel bellowed, causing Hrym to stop and look at her curiously.

"Tell me you have not fallen for her." Amusement curled at his lips and Hel wanted to slap the smirk clean off his face. It felt as though he was mocking her, somehow. "You and I both know she does not belong to our world. You may play pretend all you wish, Hel, but you must be prepared. You must know... even if the world is not ending, even if by some miracle we make it out of this alive, this will not end well for you. She is no warrior, no skjaldmær. She is just a girl."

It wasn't true. No girl could pull Hel through realms. No girl could tug the truth from Hel so easily. No girl could make Hel so patient and so utterly impatient in the same breath; so invested that she might burn the world down herself just to make sure she wasn't harmed.

"I'll ask you a final time to mind your own business, *Captain.*" The word dripped with vehemence as Hel drew close enough to intimidate him. "If we are friends, then you'll do what I ask of you. Nothing more, nothing less."

Hrym sighed, rolling his eyes and avoiding Hel's wrathful gaze. "As you wish."

She made to leave but turned before she descended the steps. "We don't know what awaits us when we reach Ísland. Will you continue to the gates with us? You and your crew?"

He pursed his lips, contemplating for a moment. "Depends. Will you stop threatening me?"

Hel smirked despite herself. "Will you stop questioning my choices regarding Maeve?"

Hrym shrugged. "Out loud, perhaps. I can't pretend I'll ever understand it, though."

"Then I will stop threatening you. Out loud, that is. I can't pretend I don't still wish to be violent toward you."

He nodded. "Then, I suppose we have a deal."

* * *

"Her spirit is dwindling. We all feel it here. She may not last the journey..."

Maeve hadn't meant to listen in on Hel's conversation. She hadn't wanted to go above deck at all after her last grim experience with the ship's captain. But she'd woken cold and alone, for a moment not knowing where she was, and she'd gone in search of Hel just to confirm all of this was still real.

And Hrym had been talking about her. About her not lasting. She'd thought the cold was from the storm and the drafty ship, but only now did she realise it went far deeper than her muscles and bones. There was a strange emptiness inside her. She felt more distant from her surroundings with each moment that passed.

She raced back down to the captain's cabin and returned to the everburning hearth, fear blossoming in her like thorny stems as the words repeated in her mind again and again.

Her spirit is dwindling...

She was so cold.

She wrapped her arms around herself, swallowing down tears as she gazed at the flames. Curiosity snagged suddenly in her brain. She had been able to feel the rain outside, but not touch objects in India's house. If she could just remind herself that this was real, that she wasn't just a ghost, a spirit, but a real person who could feel and touch and survive...

Without thinking, she stretched her hand out. The heat of the fire was little more than a tickle on her palm and it did nothing to warm her up. Biting down on a trembling bottom lip, she put her hand closer still, watching the orange glow stain her skin. She hissed at the sting, but it still felt distant.

Hel had been wrong. Maeve could feel death creeping like spiders across her back — and it felt nothing like the first time. There would be no waking up. Soon, there would be no fire, or sea, or thunder, or rain, or Hel.

Frustration guttered through her and she put her hands into the flames completely.

"*Maeve!*" Her name echoed through the cabin. Footsteps thundered across the wooden floorboards and then Hel was pulling Maeve away from the fire with bruising force. Hel's touch burned more than the flames could, the only real thing tethering her to her senses now. To anything at all.

"What are you doing?" the goddess demanded, pinning Maeve with both her hands and staring as the fire continued to smoulder behind her. "Are you *trying* to hurt yourself?"

Maeve didn't know how to answer. She hadn't been. She'd just... wanted to feel something. She'd wanted to prove Hrym's words untrue, prove she was still here, still a real person.

But even though she had felt the pain of the flames a moment ago, her skin was smooth and pale as ever. No burn, no mark; not even an echo of agony remained. It was as though it hadn't happened.

"Maeve?" Hel whispered, softly this time. Concern pinched her brow and somehow seemed to travel across the skeletal part of her face, the bones pressing and folding as though all of her was frowning.

Maeve wanted to sink into her. She wanted to beg for reassurance. Instead, she glared through her tears. "What did Hrym mean when he said my spirit is dwindling?"

Hel paled, and that said enough. She'd been stoic and stony-faced since the moment they met and now she was balking as though afraid. As though sorry. She slowly loosened her grip on Maeve's arms.

"What did he mean when he said I might not make the voyage?" Maeve's voice rose, panic setting in. She'd hoped for some explanation, some quick denial, but Hel was looking at her as though she'd seen a ghost. Perhaps she had.

Scrambling for a response, Maeve shouted, "I can't die twice! That's what you said!"

Silence, still. Hel licked her lips with a black tongue, features twisting into something unrecognisable. "You weren't supposed to hear that, Skjaldmær."

Maeve choked on a sob, turning her face away. It was true, then. "It's the reason I'm so cold. The reason I can barely feel anything. How could you not tell me?"

"I didn't tell you because I didn't want you to worry." Hel took Maeve's face in her hands, one cold and rough, the other as warm, human, as any Maeve had felt before. "Because it won't come to that. We will get you to Helheim. I will get you home. It is my only duty, my only job, and I will not fail. This is just what happens." Her breaths were heavy, but still feathered across Maeve's face like gentle fingertips. "When the spirit hasn't found a place to rest yet, it grows weaker. It doesn't mean you will disappear. It doesn't mean anything will change."

"Hrym doesn't think so," Maeve bit, fighting Hel's grip in an effort to push away.

But Hel didn't let go, and perhaps Maeve didn't want her to, not really. If this was all she got that made her real…

"Hrym doesn't know you — or me. He doesn't know

anything," Hel said. "Do you trust me?"

How could Maeve answer that? She didn't have a choice. There was no one else to trust, nothing else to hope for but that Hel would get her back in time so that she could at least try to live on, even if in a new world that wasn't hers. "I don't know."

What seemed like hurt flickered in Hel's eye. Her hands fell away from Maeve and she sat back on her feet. "Well, you should. Because I vow I will not let you slip away. I vow it, Maeve. There is not anything, not even Ragnarök, not even the end of all things, that would stop me from getting you home."

Home. Is that what Hel thought her kingdom was for Maeve? *Could* it be?

Trembling, Maeve wiped her runny nose and tried to understand the words. Understand why Hel was saying them so sincerely.

Hel's hands were fisted in her lap in defiance, in promise, tendons rippling and jaw ticking. Maeve thought of the story earlier; of who Hel was. She had been so unsure before, but now all the pieces were coming together, even if in slightly the wrong order. She'd been banished, so she had made her own home, her own realm. She surrounded herself with death so others had the chance at an afterlife.

She's protecting me.

"What will happen?" Maeve whispered. "If I do run out of time, how will I know?"

Hel's lips became a thin line. *"If,"* she said on a sigh, "you did, it would be slow, gradual. You wouldn't feel it, not really. It is more what you wouldn't feel anymore. But I won't let it happen. We have time, and you are strong."

But the world might be ending, and nobody was strong enough to stop that. She supposed if nothing else, she wouldn't be alone in her passing. Still, she would miss so much. Already did. The taste of chocolate, the smell of perfume, the sting of frostbitten skin, too quickly.

The touch of another person.

As though reading her mind, Hel found Maeve's hands. "Please believe me, Maeve," she murmured quietly. "I won't let you go."

They were just inches apart. Maeve shivered, too aware of her lips, of her swirling stomach, and that heat coiling low in her gut. As though sensing that lust, Hel swayed even closer, nose brushing Maeve's cheek. Maeve almost gasped. It was like being branded with a hot poker after so long spent numb, freezing. She needed more.

Slowly, her hand trailed from the collar of Hel's tunic to the nape of her neck. Her skin was softer than it should have been, fine hairs twining around Maeve's fingers. Hel's eye fluttered, forehead creasing as though she was confused. But she didn't pull away, instead touching Maeve like she had done once before, in India's house, when she had been so fascinated. She touched Maeve's face like she was a doll who might break, lips parted as though in awe.

Maeve didn't feel cold anymore.

She felt brave.

She closed the distance between them and pressed her lips to Hel's. It took a moment to get used to the strangeness of bone meeting flesh. Hel froze for a moment and then she was locking her arms around Maeve's waist, her kiss rough and sudden and more demanding than she'd been prepared for. Maeve submitted, leaning back and knowing that she would not fall. Not with Hel's muscular arms around her. Her torso was pressed to Maeve's, thighs slipping between thighs until she was everywhere, all over. Maeve could barely breathe, but she no longer knew if she wanted to. Not if it meant missing a moment of this.

Hel tried to pull away but Maeve tugged her hair gently. "Please, don't," she begged. "Please don't leave me cold again. I can't feel anything else. Only you."

Softening, Hel brushed Maeve's hair out of her face. "Is that the only reason you want this? Because there is no one else?"

Maeve shook her head without missing a beat. She hadn't meant it to sound like that. Like Hel was just there. She had never burned like this before, not for anyone, and she had never felt wanted the way Hel wanted her. She was lost, wandering, and Hel was her only tether.

Hel was guiding her through, keeping her somewhat alive, even if she wasn't and never would be again.

"I want you," Maeve whispered. And though she wouldn't say it aloud, she wanted to be hers. A thrill shot through her at the thought she might be; the way Hel protected her, the way she called her *skjaldmær*, the way she held her and talked to her and listened.

Hel didn't hesitate in taking her back, claiming her again and again. She splayed her hands against the small of Maeve's back, lifting her so that her legs were around Hel's waist, and Maeve fought back a groan as her core pulsed with need.

She was glad she hadn't put all that leather back on, only bothering with her tunic and leggings. Her sensitive nipples brushed against the material as she moved, sending flickers of pleasure through her.

Without warning, Hel rose to her feet with Maeve still wrapped around her, not bothering to break the kiss as she took Maeve to the blankets in front of the hearth. She lowered

Maeve onto the cushions and sank her face into the crook of her neck, placing gentle pecks there that made Maeve shiver. She arched her back, carefully loosening Hel's braid. She needed more, needed everything.

When Hel propped herself up on her elbows, her dark hair tumbling over them both, Maeve's world tilted — not the way it had on the reenactment battlefield, but in a much more vital way. Something was unlocked inside her. She wondered if that was what the fate of the Norns felt like, a key slotting into place, opening something far bigger than either of them and letting it rise into the world like smoke.

If there was no afterlife for her, if her spirit was withering away, at least she would have this, now. At least she could remember how it felt to be kissed, held, touched, by Hel.

She writhed for more, rocking her hips against Hel's thick thighs as they slotted between her own again. Hel's breath seemed to catch as she peeled up Maeve's tunic, exposing her soft, pale belly and heaving ribcage. A kiss was placed there. Two. "Skjaldmær," Hel whispered, over and over. "My skjaldmær."

A whimper escaped Maeve as Hel's mouth rose to the crease beneath her breasts and she pulled her tunic over her head, laying herself bare. She'd never been so forward in her last life, never so brave, but she'd seen the way Hel walked with such power in her giant's body and no longer felt insecure about her own curves. It only meant more of her could feel more of Hel, and God, she wanted to feel more.

She did when Hel took her breast in her mouth, sucking and licking her way up to Maeve's nipple. Maeve knotted her hands in Hel's thick, dark hair, feeling the ends snake across her skin like feathers. She reached her other hand down, desperate to feel friction between her thighs. A tear rolled down Maeve's cheek as she slipped her hand inside her leggings and soothed her aching clit with a slow finger. *How is it possible to feel nothing and everything?* If she was dead, or dying, how could her body feel more alive than it ever had before?

"Hel," she whispered with a shaky breath, already getting close.

Hel stopped and Maeve felt the agonizing absence immediately. But then their gazes were locked, Hel's mouth swollen and shiny and her heavy gaze full of worry. She pushed up, brushing Maeve's tears away with her thumb.

"What's wrong?"

Maeve shook her head, feeling silly. "Nothing. Nothing's wrong. Please don't stop."

"Maeve…"

"It feels *right*." It was a plea, and she tugged on Hel's shirt to keep her there, nudging herself against Hel's thigh again. "Let me see you, too."

Hel tilted her head, hesitating as she ran a cautious hand along Maeve's side. "I am not beautiful like you."

Maeve's heart thrummed at the word. She'd never been called that before, not earnestly. She kissed Hel's chin, her jaw, on the side that was all bone and sinew, nuzzling her face into the shadows she had once been afraid of. "I think you are. I think you're the most beautiful woman I've ever seen."

It wasn't a lie. The skeletal part of her face was a reminder of who Hel was, of the power she wielded, but also of who she refused to let people become: corpses. It was proof of her suffering, and she'd worn it so proudly from the moment they'd met. It was hard to believe she didn't see that now.

It was hard to believe that Maeve had ever been afraid to die at all if this was the face of death. If this was her afterlife. It felt more like a beginning, a *before*, and for the first time she hoped for more time in this strange new world.

Hel rose onto her knees slowly and unstrapped the countless armor and belts around her tunic, a long sword tucked into a scabbard included. She stripped away daggers carved from bones and necklaces that Maeve hoped weren't teeth. And then she removed her tunic and Maeve could only watch, stunned. The skeleton continued down one half of Hel's body while the rest of her was soft, dimpled flesh and curves like Maeve's. She could spend hours kissing those broad shoulders and that full stomach. She tried, sitting up and planting her mouth against Hel's fleshy collarbone before traveling to the other, hard one.

Hel seemed to shake beneath her and Maeve wondered if she'd ever been cherished like this before. "See?" she whispered. "Beautiful."

And then Hel crashed into her again and there was no more restraint as she pulled Maeve around her waist and sank back down onto the blankets with her bare belly brushing against Maeve's core. With gentle hands, Hel unpeeled Maeve's leggings and traced down her legs, the stripes of old stretch marks and the curve of her calf. There wasn't a part of Maeve left untouched as Hel ravished her, and all the while Maeve began to rock again, squeezing her breasts as want began to build.

Before her fingers returned to her clit, Hel brushed her nose against it and lapped with her tongue, and Maeve squirmed. "Please," she rasped. "Please, Hel. I need…"

"I shouldn't feel this way," Hel muttered, her words rumbling and vibrating so that the bliss only continued. Maeve could have come there and then with her words alone, but she was more focused on what Hel was saying. And what she was not saying. "I shouldn't, Skjaldmær. What have you done to me?"

Maeve didn't have an answer, only the same question. It didn't make sense. It wasn't her life. And yet she was settling into Hel as though it always had been; as though this had always been her destination.

Hel placed a delicate, lingering kiss on Maeve's thigh. It spoke of things neither of them were ready to talk about. Neither of them were ready to feel.

And then Hel drew her finger along Maeve's slick center, causing Maeve's vision to blur as she cried out. Begged. She could no longer keep track of what she was saying, only knew that nothing had ever felt this good before.

Hel's large hands stroked and pressed, the tip of her finger teasing Maeve's entrance. She circled her hips desperately as the tension built in her stomach. When Hel slipped her finger all the way in, Maeve came undone, her walls clenching around it. She was dizzy, pulsating, as she rode out her own orgasm until her muscles went slack and the slightest brush of her clit caused her world to turn white for a fleeting second.

After a moment of stillness where Maeve tried to regather her senses, Hel kissed up her belly again, her cheek flushed with wild heat. The other half of her face seemed lighter, less shrouded by blackness.

"What is it you say? 'Holy shit'?" Hel asked finally.

Maeve giggled. The words sounded strange coming from her mouth. "Right. Yeah. That about sums it up."

Hel smiled as though proud, sinking to Maeve's side. Maeve couldn't bear the distance and rolled over to nestle into her, though now that she was coming back to herself, she wasn't quite sure whether goddesses of death enjoyed cuddling. Still,

Hel didn't protest when Maeve hooked a leg around hers, pressing her head against Hel's chest to hear that strange, erratic hum.

Hel placed a final kiss into Maeve's hair, arranging a blanket across them both as she wrapped arms around her. And if the coldness crept back in as Maeve dozed, she no longer paid it any heed.

As long as Hel was here, she was alive.

Chapter Ten

Hel clutched the rough railings of *Naglfar* so tightly that the nails of the dead shifted beneath her palms. On the horizon, a steady billow of smoke fed into the murky, lightning-split sky, painting the world an ominous black. It seemed to have infected the sea, too. The waves were like coal tumbling under the ship, leaving the journey even rockier than it had been yesterday.

For the first time, she let herself wonder if this really was Ragnarök and a sliver of icy fear ran through her. Strange to imagine the end of days when the night she'd shared with Maeve felt so much like a beginning. This couldn't be it. After an immortal life of death, blood, pain, banishment, isolation, she had found something quite the opposite. She had never been so close with another being, never been so desperate to draw moans of pleasure out of them, kiss every spot of their skin, feel their souls tangle. She hadn't even known that so much peace and warmth and intimacy was possible.

She wouldn't let it be ripped away. She needed more. She needed to discover Maeve inside and out. Ached to.

A voice at her side made her jump.

"Can't even see Hekla behind all that smoke," Hrym grumbled, his face rain-beaten. "Are you sure we should be heading into the eye of the storm?"

The ship jolted without warning and it was an effort for Hel to keep upright as barrels and belongings slipped from one side of the deck to the other. The crew bellowed orders into the winds, the sails wracked by the force with raucous objections. One of the most powerful warships in the world suddenly felt frail. Hel thought of how she'd left Maeve in the cabin, sleeping soundly, blanket wrapped around her beautiful bare body.

Cold.

For a moment, she'd brightened in Hel's arms, but when Hel had felt her forehead before leaving her, all warmth had seeped away again. There was no other option but to risk the journey. To travel through the smoke.

"Where else is there to go?" she asked. "The storm has only gotten worse. There will be no respite until we stop whatever this is."

"Then I suppose we are following you to the death, Goddess Hel. How apt." Hrym smirked and reached out a large, rough hand.

She took it, squeezing appreciatively as they shook in silent agreement. "You might be an annoying old bastard but you're a decent man. There's a place for you and your crew in Hel if the worst happens." If she could even reach her kingdom through the smog. The gates felt further than ever now.

"I should certainly think so." He gave her a playful slap on the shoulder before returning to the quarterdeck, leaving Hel to gaze out to sea alone.

Her hunched back prickled and she heard the gentle scuff of feet against wood as the air seemed to lighten. She turned to find Maeve clutching onto any support she could find as she emerged from the captain's quarters, wrapped in Hel's cape.

Her face was bone-white, expression sickly as she made her way over to Hel on unsteady feet.

"Is everything okay?" Maeve asked.

Hel held her by the waist so that she wouldn't fall, her breath hitching in her throat as that tingling hot need returned to her stomach. Still, it was overpowered by a concern that wouldn't fade until Maeve was safe beyond Hel's gates. "Everything is…" Hel glanced in Hekla's direction again and winced. "Everything is."

Maeve's eyes widened as she followed the trail of smoke. A low gasp fell from her and thunder followed, the world shaking. She held onto Hel tightly as their feet stumbled together. "What is that?"

"That is Hekla," Hel murmured darkly. "She usually offers a far more pleasant welcome."

Remaining silent, Maeve swallowed tightly, her eyes dancing with overwhelming fear.

Hel ached. She ached because she could do nothing to comfort Maeve now. There would be no more stolen kisses or holding one another by the hearth. Not until they got through this. Slowly, she pulled Maeve into her chest and wrapped her arms around her, smoothing down her wild, silvery hair as she shielded her from the rain and winds.

"There is so much I wish to show you in Hel," she whispered. "Mountains that have stood since the beginning of everything. Waterfalls that span thousands of meters. There is so much peace to be found there. And at night my people sing and dance in the streets." She smiled, a tear rolling down her cheek, warmer than the rain sluicing her skin. She wasn't sure why, and she was glad Maeve could not see her. "I would like to dance with you, Maeve. I know you feel lost, still, and this is not your world, but I hope one day it might be."

Maeve drifted away, looking up at Hel, searching. "Hel…" She licked her lips as though there was something she wanted to say. Hel leaned forward, closer, desperate to hear it.

But it never came.

A colossal wave swallowed up the ship without warning, tilting the world and staining it grey. Maeve disappeared among the seafoam, ripped from Hel's grasp as they were chewed up by the ocean's sharp teeth.

"Maeve!" Hel's throat stung with the aggression of her shout as she was thrown to the other side of the deck, her back hitting the railings. Her skin turned to ice, mouth to salt, as she fought desperately for something to grab on to. She found a rope just as the next wave came, only just glimpsing Hrym's shocked face before she was plunged back down. This time, her boots left the safety of the deck and she could see nothing, feel nothing, her world thrown off kilter. She scrambled desperately for breath, lungs beginning to burn as she kicked and fought, but the waves kept coming and Hel could see the distorted sails sinking above in the dreary, violet sky.

Panic shot through her, not for herself, but for Maeve. She wanted to shout her name again but she choked on the water and then she was being tossed like flotsam across the waves and there was nothing. Nothing but this unending void.

Drowning. I am drowning.

She scrambled harder now, letting the current take her until finally it loosened its grip just enough for her to break free. She rose to the surface like a phoenix from the ashes, the water rippling white around her as though frightened of her power. All around her was nothing but grey between flashes of eerie lightning forks. She could just make out the last of *Naglfar's* mast sinking into the sea, its debris floating on the waves, and her stomach turned to water.

The greatest ship in Midgard, destroyed...

And Maeve...

"*Maeve!*" The panic in her voice lifted over the thunder, louder still in her own ears. "*Maeve!*"

Naglfar's crewmates began to rise to the surface one by one, but none of them bore Maeve's silvery hair. None of them were the face Hel was looking for. Despair ate at her as she imagined the worst, but there was no time, no way of gripping on to hope, as another wave tossed her back. A lifetime felt to have passed before she found the air again, spluttering on salty seawater as she searched frantically. She caught sight of Hrym waving his arms, but just as she began to swim toward him, another wave dragged her under.

This time, she was not strong enough to fight it.

* * *

Hel woke with the taste of ash on her tongue, the earth beneath her grainy and cold — but there. She pulled herself up with a start, the sound of the waves echoing in her ears. They rose and fell on the shore like the breath of a large beast in front of her, the horizon nothing more than a black line. Her bones felt like blocks of ice, leaving her numb and stiff and aching, but she paid it no heed as she remembered how she had gotten here, who she had been searching for before the sea had taken her hostage.

Maeve.

Clawing through the sand, she pulled herself onto unsteady feet, breaths falling out of her in rasps. "Maeve?" she whispered, teeth chattering. And then, as she finally straightened to search the black-sanded beach: "Maeve!"

The green peaks of Ìsland were barely visible for the mist blanketing everything. Even if Maeve was here, how would Hel find her?

No. She set her jaw in determination, refusing to entertain the other option — that Maeve was gone. If Hel had been dragged to shore, so had she. And there, in the fog, she saw the shadows of Jötnar helping one another to safety. Hrym's crew.

"*Maeve!*" Hel screamed, following the coastline. The crewmates watched as she fled past them, her salt-marked boots sinking into the sand. Still there was no Maeve. Her heart began to fall far deeper than her body had in those waves.

Maeve was lost. And without her, Hel was, too.

Hel reached the end of the beach, where basalt rose like pillars, and sank to her knees. Maeve was gone. Hel had promised her that she would take her home, give her an afterlife that would make her happy. She had made plans with her — to live and to dance and to be together the way they had on the ship last night, speaking their own language, kissing their way across one another's bodies.

And Helhest, her loyal mount, her true companion, who had taken her through centuries of death and war — gone, too. She could only assume the horse hadn't made it through the tempest. Hester had served her well for decades, centuries — it hurt to think that she would not get the chance to say a proper goodbye. That she may have died alone and afraid.

She contemplated going back into the sea, but Hel was no fool. She knew that if Maeve and Hester weren't here, they were nowhere. She couldn't even remember what Maeve's last words had been, or whether Hel had replied. It wouldn't have been enough regardless; never enough to describe how Maeve made Hel feel. How changed she was in such a short time of knowing her.

Tears rolled down Hel's cheeks as she lifted her head to the sky. If she thought it would help, she might have prayed to the gods — to Odin, even. But he was not in the business of performing miracles, and with the world as it was, she wasn't sure he'd hear.

Instead, she called for the only thing she still believed in with a guttural scream torn straight from her ocean-ravaged lungs. Her head dropped, shoulders hunched, as grief tore through her like claws. *"Maeve!"*

Her name was called somewhere nearby. She ignored it, let it wash away with the tide.

"Hel!" the low voice shouted again. She vaguely recognized it to be Hrym's, but she couldn't respond. Her body was too heavy, heart too broken, to move. "Come here, for Odin's sake! We've found your bloody mortal — and your mount!"

Hel's head snapped up, then, warmth fighting its way back between the slabs of her ribs. In the mist, she saw Hrym motioning to her before bending over a limp figure on the sand. A smaller woman. Helhest stood proudly beside them, her eyes black as the beach and mane dripping with water.

Hel rose as though tugged by an invisible piece of rope, her legs moving without her command. She didn't believe it at first, convinced she was hallucinating — until she stepped close enough to see properly. Maeve's face was pale, hair damp and splayed across the sand, eyes closed and veins visible beneath translucent skin.

A relieved sob fell from Hel as she knelt again, brushing the sand from Maeve's face. "Maeve?"

Nothing. Maeve didn't move. Her chest, too, was still.

"She was on Helhest's back," Hrym said. "She must have saved her, somehow."

It didn't surprise her. Not even Hel knew the extent of Hester's strength, though clearly she'd proven plenty today. Hel made a mental note to prepare a feast of fruit and grass for Hester when they returned home.

"She isn't breathing." Instinctively, Hel bent down, tilting her ear to Maeve's mouth in the hopes she might be wrong. But she heard nothing, felt no whisper of warmth against her skin.

"No. I'm not losing you now. Not again," she vowed, clasping her hands to Maeve's chest and pressing in firm, quick intervals. She was unused to moving with so much care, but Maeve was so small, so breakable, in comparison to the jötnar. Hrym and his crewmates watched in silence, some of them already sporting looks of grief, as though Maeve was already lost. But Hel knew she wasn't. She would carry her body to the gates of Helheim herself if she had to, but she was taking Maeve home. Alive.

"Come on, *ástin mín*," she whispered when Maeve still did not move. *My love*, a term she had never used before. It should have felt foreign on her tongue, but it didn't. It felt true. Right. And the fact hurt, because Maeve hadn't heard it. *"Please."*

She lowered, pinching Maeve's nose and breathing into her mouth. Their foreheads almost collided as Maeve spluttered into a fit of coughs and Hel sank back onto her heels in relief. Her eyes fluttered closed for a moment, tears rolling down her cheeks, before she tended to Maeve. She drew soft circles between her shoulders as Maeve coughed up half the ocean.

"That's it. Breathe," she urged. Her gaze rested on Hrym for a moment and he offered her a weak, knowing smile. She would have to thank him, but she'd save it for when the world wasn't ending.

"Hel," Maeve choked out, gripping onto Hel's tunic as though afraid to let go.

"I'm here, Skjaldmær," Hel breathed, pulling her close. She was so cold, shuddering between Hel's arms, but she was here, alive, and it meant more to Hel than she could ever articulate. "We need to find warmth, shelter," she said to Hrym.

He nodded and ordered some of his crewmates to do just that.

"I feel like I'm disappearing," Maeve mumbled into Hel's throat. "I feel so cold."

"You aren't going anywhere." It was a command as much as a promise, because she couldn't lose Maeve again. "We're almost there."

Beyond Maeve's shoulder and the beach, she took in the ash and smog chewing up the land and a shiver crawled down her spine. She had no way of knowing what waited for them. No way of knowing whether they'd survive it.

But Hel knew she would do anything to protect her home and keep Maeve safe.

Chapter Eleven

Maeve only felt tethered to the universe, to her spirit, when Hel was close. She'd realised it on the way to find shelter, Hel's arms around her, carrying her weak frame. Now, they sat by a fire Hrym had made, stuck in the shadows of a cave far too small for Hel to stand upright. She warmed her hands against the flames, glancing around. The other crewmates were outside, regrouping, so it was just the two of them. Maeve couldn't help but feel like a burden. The earth was shuddering beneath their feet and they were stuck here, waiting for her to feel able to go on as though she wasn't already dying.

"You would be better off going without me," she said finally. Her voice was still hoarse from coughing up so much seawater. It no longer sounded like her own as it echoed against the cave walls.

Hel's gaze snapped to Maeve, flaring with disbelief. "Excuse me?"

"I'm holding you back," she whispered. "All of you. I won't make it another day—"

"*Don't!*" The word was steely and sharp-edged, a general instructing her soldier. Maeve might have been frightened once, but now she knew better. If Hel was trying to intimidate her, it was only because she was scared, too — perhaps for Maeve, but most likely for her kingdom. A kingdom she wanted Maeve to be part of. "I'm getting you home. There is no other option."

"Hel..." Maeve summoned the strength to sidle closer, reaching to cup Hel's jaw. Hel's face was wary, afraid. The right side of her was as pale as the sinew exposed on the other, a blue smudge of exhaustion beneath her eye. "Your kingdom needs you. It doesn't need me."

"*I* need you," Hel bit out. "I didn't get you this far to give up now. I promised you that we would dance, that we would live, and I intend to keep that promise. No more of this, Maeve. There is nothing you can say that will convince me to leave you behind. Not after..."

Hel's throat bobbed and she looked away quickly. "I thought," she said lowly, "that I had lost you. I will not feel that emptiness again. I will not."

Maeve pressed her lips together, tears glossing her eyes both from the thick ash of the air and the heavy, all-consuming emotion she felt. She'd thought it had been the end, too, when that wave had washed them away from *Naglfar*. But then the light had flooded in and there Hel had been, hunched over her, begging for her to hold on.

There must have been a reason only Hel could keep Maeve from slipping away. Whether it was fate or the natural order of things, or whatever burned between them...

Still, it made no sense. Why Maeve? What made her so special — special enough for a goddess? "I'm just a mortal," she reminded quietly.

"You are a skjaldmær. You may not have been a warrior in life, but you can be one in death." Hel spoke with such conviction that Maeve's ribs tightened. "The Norns do not make mistakes."

"But they have, Hel." Sadness filled Maeve's voice as she tried to pull Hel back, to make her see. "Listen to me. I'm not afraid to die anymore. The little time we've had together... it meant more to me than the twenty-six years I lived before. If this is all I get, if this is all we have... that's okay with me. It's more than I could have asked for."

"Why are you giving up on me?" Hel tore herself away from Maeve's touch, her face contorting with an anger that made Maeve flinch. More than that, though, was bewilderment, bright in her eye, as though Hel truly didn't understand. "Why are you trying to say goodbye?"

"I don't want to disappear without having said it," Maeve replied. "Hrym said I don't have much time left. Even less now. I'm weak, Hel, and I'm trying to make peace with my death. Isn't that what you asked of me?"

"I'm asking you now to stop!" Hel's snarl bounced off the cave walls, dust and stone crumbled from the impact. "Now it is me who cannot make peace with it, Skjaldmær, so do not expect me to. I keep my promises!"

Maeve bit her lip, tears spilling across her cheeks. She'd never seen Hel like this: desperate. A part of Maeve wondered if she also knew how unlikely it was that they'd make it to the afterlife together. She wondered if she'd lost others like this or if her unexplained fury was another symptom of a life centered around death. Maybe it just came with the territory of being a goddess, having enough power to get anything she wanted.

Maybe she had never lost before now.

Dipping her head, Maeve wasn't sure what else to say. She closed her tired eyes, leaning back against the cave wall. Her clothes were still a tad damp, but she was slowly warming enough to feel her limbs again, even if the shivering that had plagued her for days still remained.

A sigh rustled through the cave and then Hel's leathers creaked as she moved closer again. That alone made Maeve feel more real, as though her life force depended on Hel's proximity.

A strand of Maeve's hair was brushed from her forehead. Hel said, "If you give up on me now, we will never dance. Never have the chance to be together. Do you not want those things?"

Maeve opened her eyes. Hel's features were solemn and vulnerable, a stark contrast to the guarded defiance a moment ago. Guilt twinged through Maeve. "Of course I do. I just don't want to be the reason you can't get home. I don't want to slow you down if I'm going to die either way. I want one of us to make it out of this."

"We're both making it out of this," Hel insisted. "We are so close. Don't give up on me."

Softening, Maeve twined her fingers around the nape of Hel's neck and pulled her close enough that their foreheads touched.

"Please," Hel whispered, sounding uncharacteristically meek. "Please, *ástin mín.*"

"What does that mean?" asked Maeve, tracing Hel's lips as though they might have the answers.

"'My love,'" Hel said. "'Please, my love.'"

Warmth flushed through Maeve like light and she knew now that she couldn't give up. Not on Hel. Not on hope. She kissed Hel slowly, sensation and life bleeding back into her, little by little. Hel's hands began to explore like the night before, slow and careful and fascinated. Maeve's lips roved down to Hel's neck, where she could still taste sea salt and smoke and sand. Her back pressed against the rough cave wall as Hel pushed back, rising to her knees.

"There is so much more I want to do with you," Hel rasped, her breath hot and heavy against Maeve's ear as her fingers crawled up her thighs slowly. "So much more left yet, Skjaldmær." She pressed Maeve's heat through her leggings, causing Maeve to gasp. "Tell me you're here. That you won't give up."

She'd forgotten about the crewmates outside. Forgotten about everything but Hel and her dizzying touch. Maeve had been ice cold a moment ago. Now she was on fire. "I'm here," she promised, rocking her hips to create more friction. "I won't give up. I'll fight for you."

It was a truth she hadn't considered until now; had never considered herself capable of fighting at all. But as Hel touched her, sending electricity through her bones and driving her to a shuddering, quick climax, Maeve knew she'd been a fool to give up. Hel kept her here. That there was still a home left to go to, a person to be with at the end of Maeve's life, had to mean something.

Maeve would make it mean something.

Chapter Twelve

Ísland had turned to ash. Hekla still spewed smoke and glowing, orange lava from its mouth, closer now than it had been in days. It was hard to breathe as Helhest dragged them over a land Hel once knew but now didn't recognise. Maeve's coughs rattled against Hel's chest. The crewmates trailing like loyal servants seemed to struggle just as much. Concerned, she could only wrap her arm tighter around Maeve's soft waist, inhaling the scent of her when Maeve sighed and leaned back, letting Hel place a kiss in her hair.

"We're almost there, Skjaldmær. Not long, now." Hel didn't know if it was the truth. She couldn't see anything save for the forks of lightning cutting through the cloud of dust every now and again, seeming to point into the mouth of the volcano itself. She ached from hours of riding, having slowed often to keep in time with Hrym and his crew. Better they faced this together.

Finally, the infinite, soaring branches of Yggdrasil sliced through the smog. Behind it, the Gjöll was no longer a river of water, but lava. Where once the ash tree had shone with loam and bloomed full of heavy green leaves, it was now blackened and bare.

Maeve gasped, straightening weakly. "Is that…?"

"Yggdrasil. The world tree. But something is wrong."

She didn't have time to explain. As Hester led them forward, she caught sight of three colossal figures hunched by the well beneath the tree, rapidly weaving threads as fine as spiderwebs between their fingers. They were gray with ash, from the hoods of their capes to their bare feet, but still they worked.

The Norns. The giantesses who had put Hel on this path — and every other.

The crew fell silent, stopping behind a stunned Hrym. Hel continued warily. The Norns looked up in unison when she grew close and she squeezed Maeve's hip in an attempt to reassure her. It was rare that one disturbed the Norns from their work. Hel had never tried. She supposed that if ever there was a time, these circumstances provided a good excuse.

"Goddess Hel," the front Norn, a wrinkled jötunn named Urd, regarded her as though it was perfectly natural to stand on the dying land of a fractured world. "We've been expecting you."

Hel took a deep breath, keeping Maeve steady on Hester as she lowered herself to the floor. It was difficult to tear her touch away, afraid that once she did, Maeve would disappear, but she found the courage to step down, leaving her sceptre with them.

She placed her fist on her chest as a show of respect. "*Heill þik.*" *Hail to you.* "We, on the other hand, are surprised to see you. Perhaps you can provide some guidance on what ails Hekla."

"It is nature's gift to go through phases," Verdandi, the tallest Norn, replied, growing to her full height as she paused weaving. Her eyes shone like amber like the lava running through Gjöll; always so unsettling, even to Hel. "Hekla will right herself in the end. The realms will steady again when she does. It is your

91

companion we worry about."

All three pairs of wise, glimmering eyes dropped behind Hel to Maeve and Hel's shoulders squared protectively. "I'm not certain what you mean."

"She isn't supposed to be here, Goddess." Unlike the other two, Skuld's youth had been preserved, her brown skin bright and unblemished, but her features intimidatingly firm nonetheless. She joined Verdandi behind Urd, curiosity clear as she scrutinized Maeve. "You know that."

Maeve's restless fear seemed to wind around Hel like rope, but she paid it no heed. She'd made a promise, and this was no mistake. "On the contrary. I followed the call of fate as I always do and it led me to this warrior."

"You were caught in a tear between the realms." Verdandi's features were sympathetic, an alarming contrast to her usually stern, ancient steel. "This girl is not from our Midgard, nor any other realm we weave for. She is not ours, Hel. She must go back."

Panic leapt in Hel's chest as she considered the words. All along, she'd insisted this was right; that the Fates were never wrong and Maeve was where she was supposed to be, by Hel's side. She'd been so certain that the Norns had put her on this path for a reason.

And now they were looking at her as though they knew what Hel was about to lose. As though this truly had been a mistake born not from them, but the trembling, unsteady world beneath their feet.

"You're wrong," Hel whispered. She should have been afraid to talk to the most powerful beings in her universe in such a way but she wouldn't accept their words. Wouldn't accept that, after everything, Maeve wasn't supposed to be here. "With all due respect, you are wrong. Maeve would make a fine addition to my kingdom. Even if what you are saying is true, that you never meant for me to claim her… she is here now, and I wish to take her to Hel with me."

"We cannot do that." Skuld went back to weaving as though that was it. The end of it. "We did not choose this. You'd be disrupting our threads, defying our fate, by bringing her along. Let her go, Hel. She is already fading. Let another universe decide what to do with her spirit."

"*No.*" Hel couldn't stop her snarl now. She felt the heat of Hrym at her back and thought for a moment he was going to reprimand her, or else pull her away.

But he said: "*Heill,* Norns. I don't wish to interrupt, but I must stand with Hel. The girl is strong. If our goddess believes she is worthy of the underworld, I see no reason not to let her continue to the gates."

Verdandi narrowed her eyes — they were the same shade as Yggdrasil's fallen emerald leaves. "It is not Hel's decision, Captain. It is ours. Have you forgotten?"

"Of course not." His mouth pressed into a thin line beneath his fuzzy beard.

Hel couldn't breathe.

She could not defy the Norns.

But she could not leave Maeve behind.

"*Please,*" she begged, her voice breaking, "I have never asked you for aid. Not when I was cast down, not when I rebuilt a kingdom from dust. I ask you only this, now. Let me take her to Helheim."

"That is your argument?" snapped Skuld. "You believe we owe you something?" She stepped forward on heavy feet, glowering down at Hel. She was twice her size, and thrice

93

as hard-faced, scorn burning through her.

"Skuld," Urd warned in a low voice, reaching out a hand to quiet her. Her robes whistled and mingled with drifting ash as she stepped between them. Her delicate, intertwined fingers and gray, braided hair did not belong on a jötunn, and yet she might as well have been as graceful a goddess as Sif, patience rolling off her in waves. Nothing like the fire of the others.

"You have grown attached to the mortal," she said. It was not a question.

Hel nodded slowly. "I have. I refuse to go on without her. I do not wish to defy you, Norns, for you have led me through many wars and given me a life I am proud of. But I have made a promise..." She turned back, looking at Maeve with a softening gaze. "I promised that I would keep her safe. I promised there was a place for her in my kingdom. Are you to take that from her?"

"It is not our fate to weave," Verdandi said.

"But aren't you weaving it anyway if you stop me now?" Maeve's voice, loud and clear as a river bursting across flood banks, came as a surprise. She climbed down from Hester with little grace and Hel took her hand before she stumbled and fell. A part of her wanted to say, *No. Don't speak. Leave this to me.* Another part of her was in awe. Maeve had hidden from so much of Hel's world, meek in the face of death and storms and Hrym and his giants.

Not now. Now, she set her jaw, tipped her chin as though she might be just as tall as the Norns, even if she had to look up at them. "If you keep me from an afterlife, you're still making a choice. You're still weaving my fate. I don't wish to wait here and let the universe decide. I don't wish to find out how much more my spirit can take. I want to decide my own fate — and I

94

have decided. I've decided that I want a life with Hel. I want what she's offering. I'm not asking you to weave any threads or whatever it is you do all day. I'm just asking you to let us continue."

Silence fell among the Norns. Verdandi looked uncertainly at Skuld. Urd smiled, her cheeks folding around the corners of her mouth like paper. She hummed and her skin seemed to smooth out like creases dropping from linen. Her silver hair darkened to a mousy brown, her face growing more narrow, more... *human.*

Maeve stiffened and seemed to pale. "It was *you.*"

A nod.

Hel frowned. Whatever was passing between them... it made her uneasy. "What was?"

"She... *she* is the woman who stabbed me at the reenactment," Maeve said, wide-eyed. "She is the reason I died!"

"Oh, fates." Skuld sighed and slumped as though defeated, going back to her threads. "Urd has been playing games again. Really, sister?"

Urd shrugged. "Immortality grows boring. Besides, didn't I choose right? She has softened the great goddess of death, after all. No mean feat."

Anger bubbled in Hel, her fingers curling into fists. Even Hrym looked bewildered. "*You* planned all of this?"

"How is that possible?" Maeve asked, tears sparkling in her eyes. "You said my fate wasn't yours to weave—"

"Urd likes to create threads of her own." Verdandi rolled her eyes and draped herself across one of Yggdrasil's roots, looking bored. "Last time she plucked Ragnar Hairy-breeches straight from a prison in an alternate timeline. No wonder he was such an angry fellow. At least *he* fit in well with his new era."

"Though he *was* thrown into a pit of snakes in the end," Skuld added. "You can't keep doing this, dear Urd. It isn't right, playing with universes and timelines and whatnot."

So this was what happened when fate was led by a trio of immortal jötnar with too much time on their hands. Frustrated and confused and, most of all, exhausted, Hel scraped a hand over her grimy face and tried to restrain herself. Even she was not brave enough to attack a Norn — nobody knew the true extent of their power — and she could only stand, simmering in her rage.

"You mean to tell me," she muttered lowly, darkly, "that you killed a mortal from another realm, another time, for a bit of light entertainment? All of this... could have been prevented?"

"Is that what you'd want?" Urd asked knowingly. "To have never met your mortal? I was not the only one growing bored, Hel. I watched you gather the dead, day in, day out. A passionless job, is it not? Until her, at least."

Hel wished she could say yes, she'd want that — that an innocent life wasn't worth the fullness, the fires, in her chest.

She couldn't.

She would never regret meeting Maeve. Maybe she *had* grown bored through the years, making the same trips each day to collect bloodied warriors and settling down in a hollow palace alone each night. *Hadn't the world grown tired of war?* she'd wonder sometimes. She'd kept waiting for it to; kept waiting for men to realise that there was more to living than battling for land and leadership. They never did. And eventually, she'd grown to see her people as fools. It was why she'd made her kingdom so bright and busy. To remind them that they were more than just violence. To paint their afterlife with music and dancing and celebration instead of bloodshed.

But Urd hadn't done any of this for that reason. Hel could see mischief twinkling like a star now, where once Hel had mistaken it for wisdom. She'd just wanted a game.

She thought of Maeve sobbing on the empty battlefield in Jorvik, mourning her own life. It had been taken from her without thought, without apology.

A low growl started in Hel's chest as she remembered the pain in those sobs. The fear. The heartbreak. Hel might have benefitted from this, but Maeve had lost everything she'd known. "How *dare* you?"

"Oh, enough of that." Urd waved a bored hand. "It all worked out in the end, didn't it? You should be thanking me."

"*Thanking* you?" Maeve brushed past Hel as though she was not doll-sized compared to every other being gathered around the ash tree. Hel had seen her devastated and tired and amused, but she had never seen her like this; bristling with anger, cheeks flushed, eyes sparking like two stones rubbed vigorously together. Her hair curled around her shoulders, caked in sand and ash, her face just as dirty. She looked every bit the skjaldmær Hel had believed she was. She needed only a weapon, a sword, a battlefield. Despite her own ire, heat stirred in Hel. There was so much left to discover in the woman. So many more emotions Hel wanted to see written across her body.

Perhaps not this, though. Not the dark shadows passing across her face, the tears spilling down her cheeks. "You took *everything* from me!" she raged, her voice hoarse. "My *life*! A life I deserved to *live*! For what? For fun?"

"Yes," Urd said simply; without regret, without shame.

Hel wanted to roar. She readied herself, her hand drifting to the hilt of the sword strapped around her belt — but Maeve reached out first and her lifted palm collided with Urd's chin. Shock rolled through their audience, tugging gasps from the Norns and *Naglfar*'s crew alike.

Urd's face flushed crimson as she regarded Maeve. Dread filled Hel. The slap likely hadn't hurt, but she was still a Norn. The world was hers to manipulate and she had proven that.

Before Urd could react, Hel stepped between them, Maeve's chest brushing Hel's back. She heard her breaths come out in short bursts. Urd's were still silent as though she hadn't been impacted.

"I was considering letting you go," Urd said. "Now, I'm not sure you deserve such a pleasant afterlife."

Hel's lip curled and she bore her teeth like a wild beast. She felt like one, too, her stomach jittery, body poised for battle. It had been a long time since she'd had something to fight for. She unsheathed her sword with one swift flick of her hand, readying it in warning.

"Enough, Urd." Verdandi stood again. "Let her go. Let them all go. Haven't you terrorised them enough?"

"I'm inclined to agree," Skuld chimed in, crossing her arms over her broad chest. "I'm beginning to wonder if Hekla's anger isn't reserved especially for you and your wicked games."

Urd stared for a moment longer before resigning with a huff, her face growing wrinkled and hers again. "Oh, fine. Off you go, then. Enjoy Helheim."

"*No!*" Maeve shouted, still dripping with sweat and spite.

Urd lifted her brows as though amused. "I'm sorry?"

"If you can take me out of my own world..." Maeve swallowed. It was easy to see through her bravery now. "Couldn't you put me back?"

Urd smirked again, this time directing it at Hel as though she knew what the question meant. The pain it was causing. "Is that what you wish?"

The blood drained from Hel's face as she considered the possibility. That Maeve would even ask felt like a kick in her already winded gut, though she should have known better than to believe she was Maeve's first choice. This still wasn't her life, and the Norns had all but confirmed it was never supposed to be.

Maeve gritted her teeth. "Answer my question first. Since you murdered me, I think I deserve it."

"No," Urd said finally. "There is no rewriting."

Maeve stepped back, eyes falling to her feet as though disappointed. She was still trembling as her gaze drifted to Hel. "I *told* you I wasn't supposed to be here! You didn't listen."

Hel frowned. "Even if I had, how could I prevent this? I only follow fate. I don't create it."

Shaking her head solemnly, Maeve replied in a whisper, "This isn't my fate." She returned to Helhest, clutching his reins as a dozen eyes followed her, the Norns' included.

"You did not answer my question," Urd reminded her.

"It hardly seems to matter now," she replied bitterly.

Hel pursed her lips, a chasm opening inside her. All that planning, all that imagining for the two of them... it had been Hel's making, not hers. Maeve didn't want this. She'd never been given a choice, and it was clear that if she had, she would have decided differently.

Clearing her throat of its lump, Hel glared at the three scheming sisters. "I'm not above weaving a thread of my own." She leaned in close, muttering, "And you won't like the fate I come up with for you should our paths cross again."

A muscle in Urd's delicate jaw ticked but she said nothing.

Perhaps she knew what she'd awakened by using Maeve as a toy, a beast that would tear through the world if it had to. Expression twisted with contempt, she walked backward, letting it be a warning as she slipped her sword back into its sheath.

Verdandi tilted her chin up, suddenly looking every bit as ancient as she must have been. "Be careful on your journey home, dear Hel. Consider my warning an apology on my sister's behalf."

A sharpness spiked through Hel as she halted before Hester. "And what do you warn me of?"

Verdandi shook her head. "I cannot reveal that much. I'm sorry. Just... prepare yourselves for what awaits you at the gates."

Hel sneered, spitting on the marshy ground at her feet. She wished she'd never met the Norns. Wished she'd never been awakened to the fact that they played with their fates, their duties, however they wished, picking and choosing and manipulating their threads to suit only them.

She helped Maeve onto Helhest, unable to look at her as she climbed on behind and snaked her arms around her to reach the reins. Helhest set off into a gallop without needing to be asked, leaving the Norns in her dust.

Chapter Thirteen

The earth continued to quake and storms continued to rage as they made their way upstream, following one of the ash tree's twisted roots. Maeve still seethed from Urd's confession. *She* had put Maeve on this path. She had murdered her for entertainment.

Maeve had once found comfort in the idea of fate, even if she wasn't sure she believed in it, but now, she saw it for what it was: cruel, petty, meaningless. Whatever fight she'd had in her to get to Hel's kingdom was fading fast the more she stewed over it all.

Finally, a golden bridge game into view, arching across a river of lava that was stark against a velvety sky. The heat left Maeve's vision wobbly, making her feel as though she was in a Dalí painting, the world melting and dripping like oil around her.

"No Modgud," Hel muttered behind her.

"Who?" asked Maeve.

"The guardian of Gjallarbrú, the bridge. She never leaves her post."

Maeve steeled herself as Helhest halted beneath her. She could feel the cold slowly seeping back in, and sometimes found it difficult to feel Helhest's saddle rocking beneath her when they rode. She was fading again, and it was happening quickly this time.

She no longer cared to fight it. Not if fate was working so hard to ruin her.

Hel ushered the horse around to address Hrym and his crewmates, who had followed them quietly ever since they'd faced the Norns. "It's unclear what we face now. The Norns say something awaits us, but perhaps they can't be trusted." Bitterness dripped from her tongue. "You're welcome to join us on the road to Hel, but I will understand if you wish to seek your own place in all this. You have fought through this storm valiantly and I cannot ask you to risk your lives again."

"We aren't leaving you and your girl alone now, Hel," Hrym responded without so much as a moment to contemplate, earning nods from his people. "Better you bring your army. Besides, the air is clearer and the mead stronger in Helheim."

Hel rolled her eyes but nodded. "Very well. Let's see what awaits us, shall we?" She grabbed Helhest's reins and led them toward the bridge, saying nothing to Maeve — as though she wasn't there.

Soon, perhaps she wouldn't be.

* * *

The sky darkened the closer they got to the gates, the world narrowing to black stone and long-dug graves of Hel's dead. Smoke engulfed them as they wound their way down, distorted shadows of the woods and hills creeping across the road like claws. Hel was no longer too proud to admit she was afraid. The trees that usually lined the journey out of Hel were bare and charred, and even from here, she could hear the distant keen of Garmr's wavering howls. It had been a stark image to find Gjallarbrú without its guardian. She could only hope Modgud had run to Helheim for shelter, and not because the Norns were right about the threat they faced at the gates.

There were hours left to go, still, and though the thunder was easing, the sky was still raining ash. She could barely breathe herself, but Maeve... her chest shuddered with shallow intakes against Hel's own, and she was paler than on the beach. Bluer, too, and barely able to hold herself up.

Hel closed her eyes, feeling a sharp pang of pain. Being close to Maeve wasn't enough anymore, and she thought she knew why.

"I'm sorry," Maeve whispered finally. "For blaming you for this. I'm sorry."

"Save your breath," Hel muttered, her voice cold even to her own ears. But she couldn't keep doing this; keep caring this much for somebody who was settling for the only fate they had left.

"You're angry with me," she pointed out between a dry, heaving cough.

Hel resisted the urge to help, instead silently offering her flask, filled with barely a few drops of water they'd collected from some springs. Polluted with ash, no doubt. She'd also insisted Maeve wear her cape, all too aware that her shivers had returned once more.

Taking the flask, Maeve sipped and wiped her mouth. "You're not talking to me now?"

"I have nothing to say." Hel tried to keep her voice low, slowing Helhest down with a pull on the reins so she could be heard over her pounding hooves.

"I'm trying to apologize. And I'm also trying to stay alive for long enough to live out the rest of my life with you. Maybe you could…" Another fit of coughs that left Maeve bent over. Hel gritted her teeth and pulled Hester to a stop, hating that she had to choose between distancing herself and letting Maeve die or helping her while knowing that nothing they shared meant nearly enough to her.

She'd seen it before. Maeve's condition eased when Hel was there with her, whether making love to her or trying to force breath back into her lungs. But she didn't feel much like doing either of those things, so she got down from her horse and lifted her arms to Maeve.

"We'll take a break. Hrym, you go on with your crew."

The instruction left Hrym looking wary but he nodded and led on, further into the shadows. Some of the crewmates had already brought out their weapons, ready for the battle the Norns had promised.

Maeve slumped into Hel's arms and that was how she knew Maeve was giving up. Hel's anger flooded back: for the Norns, for Hekla and her destruction, for everybody. She needed that vicious woman who had been willing to raise her hand to Urd back, or at least needed the grieving, confused Maeve of Midgard. But she was flat now. Empty. Difficult to read and even more difficult to reach, and Hel was *trying*. She was trying not to want her, not to need her. Trying to understand that this had never been an equal choice, an equal relationship.

But she would still catch Maeve when she was dwindling to nothing. She would pull her from the waves again and again if it meant she was here for another second, minute, hour.

She'd been carved out and made weak, and she hated that most of all. *Is this what the Norns want? Does it make them happy to watch me, a goddess, stumble to my knees because of a mortal who may not make it to the afterlife?* She wished then that she could go back, plunge her sword straight into Urd and make her pay for what she'd done. It was too late, though. There was nowhere to go but forward.

But for a moment, they would have to stand still.

Lowering Maeve to the ground, Hel helped her find her feet, leading her to the closest rock with her arm around her waist. Maeve collapsed onto the rock, coughing as she disrupted more ash. Hel only glared into the smog. She had never felt so lost.

"You must be angry with them, too," Maeve said eventually, sipping more water. "With Urd, at least. You thought you were getting a warrior. Instead, you're stuck with me."

Hel clenched her jaw and said nothing, afraid it might all come pouring out. That she was glad to be stuck with Maeve, but Maeve would rather be anywhere else.

"Shouldn't the gods be here, helping?" Maeve continued.

Hel sniffed in amusement. "The gods wouldn't lower themselves to come here. They'd sooner watch the world burn than leave Asgard."

"Even... even your father?"

Hel couldn't answer that. Instead, she dug her toe into the stone and braced herself against a warm wind, swirling through the ash and causing dead leaves to rustle.

"Hel," Maeve whispered, a plea. "Please look at me. Please."

Hel directed her glare at Maeve, her nostrils flaring. She wanted to scream. She wanted to cry. She wanted to get home and be left alone, where she couldn't be hurt.

"I don't want to die with you angry at me." Maeve's words sharpened.

"That is your choice to make!" Hel bellowed finally, erupting like Hekla herself.

Maeve frowned, shrinking slightly. "What?"

"You may not have chosen this, me," Hel spat, "but *you* choose if you live or die." She prodded a finger into Maeve's shoulder, and it was like plunging into Niflheim's icy river. "Haven't you figured that out? You recovered on *Naglfar*, enough at least to feel better. You came back to me again in the cave when I begged you to stay. *You* choose, Maeve. So if you do not wish to die with me angry at you, then you shall just have to not die!"

Maeve's mouth bobbed open, closed, as silence thickened the already suffocating atmosphere. Finally, she quipped, "I hadn't thought of just 'not dying', actually. Thank you for the advice."

Hel scoffed, turning her back before she let her rage blossom into something far more vicious. "Are you done feeling sorry for yourself? May we carry on now?"

"Feeling *sorry* for myself?" Maeve repeated incredulously. "I'm *grieving*! I lost my life, I lost myself, and for nothing! Because some giant lady by a tree decided she was bored! I'm so sorry if that's inconvenient for you. I'm so sorry I'm not you're bloody 'skeldmur' or whatever it is you want to keep calling me! But this is me, Hel. This is who you asked to come home with you. If you don't like it, maybe I shouldn't bother!"

"Then don't!" Hel growled, spinning around on her heel. The rocks around her seemed to shake and she wasn't sure if it was Hekla's doing or her own. "Don't bother. Give up as you have always done! Turn to ash with the rest of the earth, if that's what you wish!"

Maeve flinched and Hel knew she'd gone too far, dug too hard. She had never been one to fight half-heartedly, but she had forgotten for a moment *why* she was fighting and with whom. She'd forgotten that, before this, there had been gentle kisses and a steady flame burning between them.

Now, everything was on fire.

Tears sparkled in Maeve's eyes — but they were brighter than they had been. All of her was, color flushing her cheeks again. Hel was tugging the fight back out of her, and it was keeping her here, alive.

For once, it didn't feel like enough.

"I won't keep convincing you to live," Hel murmured finally. "I am sorry for what you have lost, but I won't."

"Then go." Maeve pointed toward the dark valley and fog with a trembling hand. "Go on. Leave me here. Let the Fates decide one last time what'll happen to me."

Taken aback, Hel could only stare. She wanted to — or, at least, she wished she wanted to. Life would be so much easier if she left Maeve here and never thought of her again.

"You don't understand, do you?" she asked. "The Norns put you on this path, but they haven't taken away your choice. If you stay here, you will fade away. If you choose the afterlife, you will stay. That is how it works. Your life was taken from you, and it was awful, cruel, wrong, but your choice about what happens next, what you want... that is still yours and yours alone."

Maeve's face creased in confusion as she processed Hel's words, absently running her finger through the ash covering the rock. "It doesn't feel that way."

Hel had no response to that. She closed her eyes, defeated and aching. "Let me know when you decide what you want."

She readied Hester to mount her again, taking her time because a part of her still yearned for Maeve to say it: *I choose you.*

But she didn't, and when Hel turned around, half-afraid she was about to say goodbye, she found Maeve with her knees pulled to her chest, her face tilted to the black, ruined sky. Tears mingled with dirt and tracked down her face.

"I want you to look at me like you care for me again," she finally admitted. "I want just one thing in my life to be clear. I want to know what I'm supposed to do and how I'm supposed to do it. I want to know if, by following you, I'm signing myself up for a life where I never belong. I want to know why you're so bloody angry at me all of a sudden. If it's because of this, because I'm weak, then fine. But I was always weak. *Always.* I thought even then you saw me as more than that."

She didn't understand why Hel was so hurt. She could not make the easiest decision in the world: to live or die. "It isn't about you being weak. I do not think you are weak."

"Then what is it about?"

Hel shrugged, armour rattling. "You wouldn't choose me." A pained, mangled breath fell from her. "I've chosen you over and over and you would not choose me."

A frown. "*What?* I have chosen you. I trusted you—"

"You asked Urd if there was a way to go back to your own life," Hel interrupted. "You made it clear that if there was, you would have taken it without even a moment's hesitation." She lowered her gaze. "I care for you. I feel things for you I have never felt before now. But I cannot be the thing you settle for because I am your only choice. I cannot be loved in halves because your 'what ifs' cannot come true."

Guilt sifted across Maeve's face. She was growing pale again, but not like before. "Hel—"

"You need to part with your old life if you wish to be part of mine. I understand that it's difficult and painful and you never asked for this. But neither did I, Skjaldmær. Yet, I choose you anyway. I would choose you again and again, in any circumstance, in any thread of fate. When you can say the same... that is when we can have that life I promised you. The one where we dance and laugh and lose ourselves in one another. Until then, I can't..." She sniffed as emotion settled behind her eyes like heavy weights. "Until then, I just can't," she said.

Maeve pursed her lips and Hel couldn't look at her anymore; not when sadness was written across every inch, every corner, of her. The earth rumbled again, this time as loud as though they were standing in Hekla's center. Hel made to go back to her horse, sadness welling inside her — but movement snaked across her periphery and she froze.

It wasn't the earth that was shaking. It was the graves.

"Hel—"

"Shh!" Hel ordered, lifting a finger to silence Maeve. She backed closer to her carefully, watching the soil around the vine-covered headstones tremor and roll. She felt as though she was buried beneath it, suffocating with dread and rattled by fear. "Don't move. Don't speak."

"Why—"

A mottled, blue-grey creature burst from its grave, all bloated flesh and unseeing eyes. Hel hadn't seen such a thing in years.

Draugr.

Hel pushed Maeve back, stumbling over her own feet as she took in the living corpse. It hovered over its grave, slotting its rotting bones into place before finally, slowly, turning its head to them at an unnatural angle. Patches of wiry hair stood erect on its spotted head and crooked chin, the stench of decomposition filling Hel's senses until the ash seemed harmless in comparison. She prepared her bone sceptre, eyes darting for signs of more. Another grave trembled behind them, the road to Hel lined with the bodies of warriors who had wanted a proper burial.

The bodies of warriors who were now monsters.

"What is that?" Maeve whispered, voice trembling.

"Draugr. Undead." Is this what the Norns had warned? Had Hekla disrupted the dead and awoken Hel's corpses?

One or two were easy to fight, but hundreds lived on this road and the crew would be yards ahead by now — hopefully better prepared than Hel.

As another skeletal figure crawled from its grave, Hel sucked in a deep breath and considered her options. Slowly, she unsheathed her sword, meeting the eyes of the first Draugr as she handed it over. "Take it. Aim for the chest or the head."

"I don't know how to use—"

"Then learn quickly," Hel hissed, shoving the onyx hilt into Maeve's hands. There was no time. The Draugr was staggering toward them. Hel adjusted her stance, protective in front of Maeve, her knuckles turning white around her sceptre. When the corpse was close enough, she lunged point-first.

The world turned to sour, tar-like blood and foul stenches as she tore through gristle and tendon, aiming right for the neck, but as the Draugr fell and she whipped around, she found two more already making their way toward them. Maeve turned, letting out a frightened whimper as she held the sword in front of her.

"Get behind me. Only use it if you need to," Hel instructed, pushing her back again as she swung and drove the pointed bones of her sceptre into the corpse's temple. It stumbled back, but the cut hadn't been deep enough. There was no time. The other neared and Hel grunted as she drove her boot into its stomach, adjusting her grip. In the distance, Garmr's howls turned to wails and Hel could only pray she'd make it to the gates.

She plunged through the injured one's skull, this time hitting long-dead brain matter that splattered across the ash and stone in streaks of brown and black.

"Hel!" Maeve's call cut through Hel's focus and she was thrown to the ground by a corpse not much shorter than her. It snapped its teeth at her like a starved beast, digging its bony fingers into Hel's neck as Hel writhed beneath it. She'd dropped her scepter in the scramble, she could only do her best to push the Draugr away with desperate shoves. If she couldn't get free, Maeve was on her own and all of this was for nothing.

She bellowed in an attempt to gather the last of her strength — but then her vision was painted red as a wink of silver tore through the Draugr's chest. The corpse slumped, lifeless once more, bleeding all over Hel's armour.

Above her, Maeve towered like a proud Asgardian, the sword clutched between her fists and her face streaked with dirt and blood as she gasped for breath.

"I did it," she whispered. Hel could have sworn her cheeks glowed pink with a life the Draugrs would never again possess. "I..." — she drew the sword out of the Draugr and let it clatter to the ground, wiping her forehead with her loose sleeve — "I think I'm going to throw up. Can dead people throw up?"

Hel swallowed her awe as best she could, pushing the dead Draugr off and looking around. No more signs of them, although she doubted that would be the last of them. "Are you hurt?" she asked, shaking herself off and examining Maeve.

Maeve shook her head, her face growing pale as she stepped forward. She rested her hands on Hel's shoulder and Hel winced at the fiery pain that ran up her neck. "You're bleeding."

They were so close, Maeve's warm breath fanning across Hel's skin as her eyes filled with worry. For a moment, Hel forgot everything but how it had felt to kiss her, wring pleasure and moans out of her, and that tenderness reserved only for Maeve came rushing back.

She had to remind herself that it couldn't be that way. Not now.

"Just a cut," she said with a shrug, stepping away and gathering her scepter beside the other Draugr's corpse. She dabbed her neck and her palms came away bloody. Still, she'd had worse.

"Hel..."

"We need to get back to Hrym. There'll be more Draugr along the way. Better we stick together." She unbuckled her leather weapons belt, throwing it over to Maeve without daring to look at her. "Keep the sword."

And then, because she couldn't pretend as though she wasn't impressed, as though seeing Maeve wielding her weapon so confidently hadn't confirmed something that Hel had long known about her, she added, "*Skjaldmær*."

Maeve could no longer claim weakness. She'd had a warrior's heart from the beginning — vulnerable when needed, strong when desperate.

Maeve flickered with surprise before looking down at the belt. It was far too wide to fit Maeve's waist so she slipped the sword back into its scabbard before slinging it across her shoulder.

She had never looked more herself, or perhaps, it was just Hel's wishful thinking. Projecting all the things she'd hoped Maeve had been onto the real version of her.

Somewhere inside, though, she was sure it was more than that. Maeve was only just getting to know herself.

112

Perhaps everything had changed now.

Chapter Fourteen

They found Hrym and his crew battling a swarm of Draugr not far down the road. Maeve couldn't pretend as though she wasn't terrified, even when the threat had passed and her sword was sheathed again. This time, Hel had kept her back from the fight, letting the crew take care of them. It was clear they'd all been rattled by these creatures, and she couldn't blame them — they were like something out of a horror movie, though no CGI effect could achieve half the grotesqueness their rotting flaps of skin and muscle could.

"Is it like this all the time here?" she whispered when they rode on Helhest soon after. The roads had been cleared again, for now, but it was clear from Hel's tension that she expected more cadaverous monsters to spring from the ground like withering flowers. "All those graves…"

"The dead don't wake like this often," Hel replied, keeping her cautious gaze on the unsteady soil. "I suspect Hekla's eruption is the cause. But no. If you're asking if you'll have to fight corpses every day, the answer is no. You would be safe behind the gates."

Would. Not *will.* Hel had been so certain Maeve's fate lay in Helheim before, but now… doubt lingered on the edges of her tone and Maeve knew she'd put it there herself. She hadn't thought about the implications that asking Urd for a do-over would mean when it came to Hel. She hadn't even realized Hel could be so sensitive, so passionate. Of course, they'd shared something special on the ship, but she was still a goddess.

She can't truly want me, can she?

She closed her eyes and visions of gnarled limbs and blackened teeth flashed behind her lids. She wasn't sure she'd ever sleep again.

The sound of an eerie howl rent through the air and Maeve jumped.

"That's only Garmr, my hellhound," Hel said gently. "He guards my gates."

"Oh, only a hellhound," Maeve muttered wearily, the sarcasm not lost on her. "Bear in mind I'm used to house cats who like to cuddle."

"Garmr likes to cuddle sometimes. When he's in a good mood."

She smirked despite herself but it quickly fell when she heard a snapping of tree branches. Immediately, three of Hrym's crew crossed the treeline and Maeve caught the sight of a blade burying into a yellowed, milky eye through the dead leaves. Another Draugr.

"It's okay to be afraid," Hel whispered. "This isn't how I hoped your arrival would turn out."

"I wasn't exactly expecting fanfare." It was difficult to remind herself that this place wasn't the same Hell she'd learned about as a child. There was no fire — well, save for the lava they'd trailed away from — and no devils. Only a fierce goddess and a loyal following and whatever waited on the other side of the gates. It was no longer that unknown she was scared of. It was this one. So much so that she hadn't thought about how weak her spirit felt for hours.

She sighed, missing the comfort Hel had once been able to bring her. She missed the weight of those large hands on her hips, missed kisses placed in her hair. Yesterday she'd been falling into a serenity she'd only dreamt the afterlife could bring her, and now... now, she wasn't sure if it would ever be that way again. She couldn't give Hel all of herself. She couldn't be happy that she'd left her own world behind without a goodbye. She needed to be allowed the space to grieve, and she needed Hel to know it didn't make Maeve's feelings for her any less real.

If they even *could* be real in a world of fate and Norns. The question still played on her mind; *How much of this did the Norns weave in their threads? How much of this has been decided for me by someone else?* Had Urd manufactured their feelings for one another as part of her game? It would make sense. A lost mortal and a goddess of death was hardly a believable love story.

She tried to straighten, to be strong, because when Hel had called her Skjaldmær again after she'd killed the Draugr, Maeve had wanted to believe that perhaps she could be one day. She thought of her desire to be Brunhild, to get lost in that alter-ego where she could be important and strong. Hadn't she always wanted this?

Her gaze fell back to the graves. Some of them were freshly dug up, promising Draugrs to come and sending a shiver down her spine. Others were unmoving, looking ancient and weathered, covered in bramble and weeds and ash. She'd wanted to be a warrior because she hadn't known there would be monsters to face. Everything was different now.

"Why do you keep these graves? Are the bodies people who didn't make it into Hel, or...?"

"No. The opposite," Hel said, adjusting her seat so that her thighs brushed against Maeve's. "Some would not get a burial otherwise, so we bring their bodies here before their spirits cross the gates. That way, they know where their bones lie long after they have use for them. It brings them comfort. Some believe it helps them to pass through the gates safely."

Maeve tried to imagine her body in one of those graves. It made her nauseous, though she supposed Hel's world was not one filled with glossy, expensive coffins and urns. Not that they sounded much better. For the first time in a while, she thought of her own world; where her old body might be, who might attend her funeral, what it might be like. She felt so removed from it now, even as images of India and her parents standing around a casket flooded her mind.

Whatever body rested in York, it wasn't her anymore. This was her now. The sooner she accepted it, the easier it would be.

"You are thinking of your own body," Hel commented knowingly.

Maeve nodded. "I hope they cremate me," she decided. "I want to be scattered somewhere nice. I want at least a part of me to be free."

Maeve felt Hel's brows furrow without having to look. "You don't think you're free now?"

"That's not what I meant," she said quietly. "Just… in life, I never knew who I was. I wanted to travel, but I also wanted to stay at home. I wanted to love, but I was afraid to be loved. I wanted to be successful, but I had no idea what career I wanted to pursue. Thinking of myself as ashes like the ones falling from the sky now… it takes away those tethers and insecurities. I don't want to be a corpse like these… Draugr. I want to be part of the world. I want to be part of the wind and the soil and the sea rather than stuck beneath the earth. Does that make sense?"

A few moments passed. "Perfect sense," Hel whispered. "For what it's worth, nobody can take away what you offered to the world, even if your time was cut short. You'll always be part of it. I find that often; I go to warriors whose partners shed tears, their stories of kindness and honour told around bonfires years after. I have no doubt, Maeve, that you will be someone's story for a while. And if not, you will certainly always be mine."

Maeve twisted to glimpse Hel's sadness-softened features and tears blurred her vision as her lungs tightened. Maybe she'd been wrong. Hel might have been fierce, but she was also intelligent, emotional, kind. She should not have been known as the goddess of death, not when her heart was so big. Goddess of life would have been more apt.

For a moment, Maeve imagined herself saying no to Urd's question. She couldn't imagine going back to not knowing Hel, not being near her.

Hel had to know that.

She opened her mouth to tell her but Hel's name being called with a new sense of urgency interrupted her. Twisting back around, she found a raven-haired, armour-clad woman, far daintier than Hel, standing in front of them. Helhest stopped and Hel jumped off the horse without warning, running straight into the arms of the woman.

"Modgud," she breathed, relief wavering in her voice.

The guardian of the bridge, Maeve remembered, softening as she watched the interaction. She felt as though she was intruding, but seeing Hel greet her friend as though she was unsure she'd ever get the chance again warmed something in

Maeve. And when Modgud looked back through teary eyes... it occurred to Maeve that she wasn't the only person in the world who saw Hel for what she truly was. Hel might have been terrifying and reserved sometimes, but she let the right people in. She gave them a chance. She made people's lives better, and that's exactly what she was trying to do now. For Maeve.

"I wasn't sure you were ever coming back to us," Modgud said, stepping back to take in their cavalry. Her eyes, which were almost as dark as her sweat-crusted skin, drifted to Maeve. She examined her for a moment, and while Maeve might have shrunk once, now she remained steadfast, her jaw aching from how hard she'd been clenching it. "I'm glad to see you bring a skjaldmær home with you this time. There are too many men in this kingdom for my liking."

To Maeve's surprise, Hel grinned wolfishly — proudly, almost. Maeve couldn't pretend she didn't also feel a happy flutter in her belly at being mistaken for a true warrior.

"This is Maeve."

Hrym coughed dramatically.

Hel rolled her eyes. "And you already know Captain Hrym of *Naglfar*."

"Unfortunately," Modgud muttered, her gaze returning to Hel with warmth and fondness. "I assume you know about the Draugr." She brushed her finger against Hel's wounded neck. "Nasty little vermin. Garmr has been holding them off by the gates, but... there are so many of them."

"More than there are of us?" Hrym asked.

"Dozens more. We've only been able to hold them off, but we barely made a dent in their army."

"We're here now," Hel reassured. "What about Helheim? How are my people?"

"Completely unaware that the world has been crumbling down around them, as always. Too drunk on mead and good food to pay much notice to anything else."

Hel's smile only grew wider at that and Maeve saw it then; she loved her kingdom, her people. Her world had never just been about death. It had been about them.

And I can be one of them if I would just let go...

"Let's keep it that way, shall we?" Hel pulled out her sceptre, squeezing Modgud's shoulder before climbing back onto the saddle behind Maeve. Already, she felt lighter, more relaxed.

Ready, no doubt, to fight — and win.

Chapter Fifteen

"Dozens" had been an understatement. As they reached the gate, Garmr's bright-red eyes just visible and his snarls curling through the shadows, Hel estimated at least forty Draugr to be streaming from graves and treading across the road. Some of them were attacking each other, disoriented from being dragged back to life so suddenly. Others were making headway toward the gate, where they were met with Garmr's ferocious teeth and claws. But there were too many for one wolf alone, and Hel readied her sceptre. She helped Maeve down before dismounting herself, adrenaline already humming through her — and fear, too. Maeve might have managed to kill one Draugr, but Hel knew how battles went. Some of these corpses were huge, vicious in their thirst for anything they could attack. They'd risen for no other reason than to kill, nothing more than empty bodies ready to destroy, and some of them would be stronger, faster, than Maeve.

"You could hide in the underbrush away from all this," Hel said, searching for a quiet place in the woods.

But Maeve shook her head. "I might not have been a warrior when you met me, but I want to earn my place—"

"Maeve—" she began to protest, but was quickly cut off.

Maeve cupped Hel's jaw, her eyes soft, palms burning. "I

didn't choose this, but I'm choosing now. I'm choosing to live, to fight — for *you*. Let me do it. Please." Her teeth chattered, but still she wouldn't back down. Braver than any skjaldmær Hel knew, because she was the most afraid and yet still willing to go into battle.

"I'd rather you not choose me and be safe." Nothing was worth losing Maeve. Even if Hel was only loved in halves, she could manage as long as Maeve lived. "This isn't what I meant when I asked you to fight."

"I know what you meant." She tugged the sword from its scabbard, letting it swing down at her side. It spanned from her ankle to hip and surely must have been too heavy... but she wielded it proudly nonetheless as she inched closer to Hel. "I'm scared. I'm lost. But I'll fight with you anyway because that's what I want."

Hel sighed, her heart hammering in her chest. "If you get hurt, you run," she commanded. "If it gets to be too much, go. I'll come and find you afterward. Stay behind me, or somewhere I can see you. And please... *please* be safe."

More howls erupted and Hel saw the Draugr were only getting more violent in their attempt to seize Hrym's crew. They were running out of time, and there was so much Hel wanted to say but didn't know how. She pressed her lips to Maeve's, and though she couldn't linger nearly as long as she wanted to, it was enough to know that Maeve did care, did love her.

She kissed back with a ferocity that took Hel off guard, her fingers knotting in Hel's tangled hair. "Yes."

And then a Draugr neared, and Hel pushed away, her features molding into something else entirely. Deadly determination. Vicious strength. Maeve had been afraid of it once. Now, she seemed to be in awe.

The battle began.

* * *

Maeve had been sure she would cower and run like a child, but as the Draugr flocked toward them, something in her stiffened like a lion ready to pounce. For days, she'd been ebbing in and out of her own being, her own existence, but now she was certain she could feel the ground meeting the soles of her boots. Whether it was just her body remembering or her spirit strengthening, she didn't know, but she tightened her grip around the hilt of the heavy sword, feeling the throb of her muscles like a song through her veins. She could do this. She watched Hel dive into the fight and knew she didn't want to run, didn't want to be anywhere but here, where she knew the person she was most tethered to was safe.

Not just safe, but making the unsteady earth bend to her will. She was dynamite in the midst of the clambering corpses, swiping and swinging and stabbing without missing her mark once so that bodies fell and flew and dissipated. But there was no time to admire Hel's work. Maeve had her own army to fight. She found herself screaming as she cut through the first Draugr, the squelch of tearing flesh and bone making her falter for just a moment. The Draugr collapsed on her sword, motionless. Gone.

"Holy shit."

She sucked in a deep breath and did it again. Again, again, again. More bodies thumped to the floor, more blood and rotten flesh splattered everywhere. Her sword was dripping with it, and her clothes too. She didn't stop, not as anger rose up and she saw something else in the faces of the dead. Urd, with her young, uncaring features. Suddenly, these corpses were not just monsters anymore. They were all the Fates that had brought Maeve here, all the moments in life she'd never had control over — her last heartbreak, the jobs she'd never been able to hold down, the people who had sneered at her for being lost in daydreams. The reenactment. She had not been able to fight in life, instead taking the beating every time, right until its last, deadly punch. But she could fight back now. She could win. She would never let the world decide who she was again. She would never have to pretend to be someone else.

She was Maeve. Skjaldmær and mortal, dead and alive, afraid and brave, angry and in love, a mingling paradox of all the ways she'd chosen herself since the day she'd been killed. Her life hadn't been taken, she knew now; she'd just been given a new one. She wouldn't waste it.

Still, in her determination, she hadn't seen the three Draugr coming from behind. As she slayed the one in front, she felt the grasp of skeletal fingers at her back, digging as though trying to uncover something buried beneath her skin. She cried out in pain, whipping around to face them and swinging her sword in an arc like a dancer pirouetting across the floor.

The heads slipped off their necks one by one and the bodies collapsed a moment later.

Gone.

Maeve gasped for breath, a wave of disgust catching her off guard. Corpses littered the floor. Garmr was tearing into one's shoulder as though he enjoyed the taste and Hrym's crew was bloody as they finished off the remaining few.

She caught Hel's gaze, sticky with sweat and relieved that it was over.

And then she smiled. Hel returned it, crooked teeth flashing in the darkness. She began walking to Maeve, her eyes gleaming.

Maeve took a step, too, ready to tell Hel that she had made her choice. That she understood who she was now.

She faltered when she caught the looming silhouette approaching Hel from behind, smile slowly wiped from her face. This Draugr towered over all of them, and yet somehow there was no sound of its footsteps striking the ground.

"Hel!" Maeve shrieked — too late. The Draugr lunged, knocking Hel to the floor with a hungry snarl as it clawed through her armor. Blood seeped through her linen quickly, only a touch redder than the sticky tar of the undead. Hel's. "No!"

She didn't think, didn't breathe, didn't see anything but Hel on the ground, unable to grab her lost sceptre in time to defend herself. Maeve's feet carried her and then she swung back her sword. The steel beat through the air like wings as she struck the Draugr, piercing through its torso. It wasn't enough. The Draugr only roared in anger, twisting to find Maeve. It pounced on her, and she stuck her blade into it again, flinching against the reek of death and the snapping of its teeth so close to her cheek. Its fingers embedded themselves in her shoulder and she cried out, dragging her blade up from its ribs and earning an inhuman, guttural wail. Just as the Draugr tucked its teeth into Maeve's arm, a bone-white spike broke through skull and skin and finally laid the monster to rest.

The world went eerily quiet as Maeve slumped beneath the corpse, finding Hel standing above her like a statue carved from marble, all rippling muscle and ferocity as she tore her sceptre out of flesh. A metallic stench filled Maeve's nostrils as it bled on top of her and then she was scrambling to be free, the weight of the dead too much to bear.

Hel rolled the body off with a kick of her foot and kneeled. Maeve's eyes were wide, fear still thundering through her. She'd thought that was the end. That she'd never get the chance to tell Hel how she felt, how important she was to her.

Gritting her teeth, Hel ripped one of her shirt sleeves and wrapped it around Maeve's arm with trembling fingers. She muttered something low; a curse.

"It doesn't seem fair that I can still bleed," Maeve whispered, realising that she was, in fact, wounded beneath Hel's makeshift tourniquet.

So was Hel; blackened blood gushed from her collarbone in a steady stream, a serpent slithering from its shelter.

"It doesn't seem fair that *you* can still bleed either," Maeve added, concern rushing through her. "Are you okay?"

"Fine," Hel breathed, her eyes narrowed on Maeve's wound as she clumsily tied the knot. "Because of you, I am fine."

Maeve drew her attention away long enough to see the Draugr had finally fallen — all of them. Hrym and his crew slowly began tucking away their weapons and tending to one another's wounds. Modgud stroked Garmr with a bright grin as he wagged his tail, licking blood from his lips.

She looked to the sky, then, and found it a lighter, more watery gray than it had been in days, as though the cloud was finally thinning, unveiling the world once more.

"Is it over?" She almost didn't want to believe it. Almost couldn't.

But Hel looked up beyond the bare overhanging tree branches and said, "It's over."

The ground didn't crumble or tilt. The thunder didn't roar.

Lightning no longer sliced through the sky.

Everything was still, calm.

"You fought like a true skjaldmær," Hel said, brushing her knuckle across Maeve's cheek. It came away red. Her brows furrowed. "You sacrificed yourself for me. Saved me."

Maeve leaned forward, tilting Hel's chin up gently. "Of course I did. I couldn't lose you. I…" — her nerves jittered, but she forced out the words — "I think I might love you."

Hel melted into her like syrup. "I'm sorry for all of the promises I've broken. I told you you would be safe—"

"It isn't your fault."

"I was impatient with you. I'm sorry for that, too. You deserve time to adjust, time to grieve your life. I know that. Of course I do."

"Hel," Maeve begged, desperate now for her to understand, "none of that matters now. We made it home, and this is where I want to be. With you. If you'll still have me, that is."

The corner of Hel's mouth dimpled with a smile, such a contrast from the other half of her. But Maeve had grown to love both parts just as much. She'd thought her face monstrous once, but now she knew it perfectly represented Hel's untamed, warring spirit. Death and life. Not only that, but it proved that there was no fear in either. That both were beautiful in their own ways — because she'd made it so.

"Do you honestly think I would say no, ástin mín?"

"I really hope not, because I can't say I have many other plans for the afterlife," Maeve whispered. "Just you. And dancing. You promised dancing."

Hel pressed a delicate kiss between Maeve's brows. "There will be plenty of dancing." She stood, then, holding out her hand. "Come on. Let's go home."

Maeve swallowed and looked around as though she might find something different than the corpse-eaten road and the strange landscape. As though she might be back in India's apartment with Loki the cat, waking from a nap.

That life was behind her now. It had moments of beauty in it, too, but she'd also never truly felt herself there. Not the way she did here, with Hel.

She took Hel's hand and rose to her feet, stopping to say a silent goodbye to everything she was leaving behind as the warm wind rustled through her hair.

Hel smiled sadly as though she knew, tracing figure eights into Maeve's knuckles. "Take all the time you need."

Maeve did, and in the end, it was only a second or two more. Then, she turned away from the winding road, finding that Hrym's crew had parted so she had clear access to the golden gates.

She walked toward them, not because she didn't have a choice, but because she was ready to rest with the goddess, the woman, the warrior, she had fallen in love with.

Chapter Sixteen

The gates drew open slowly, Garmr nudging the elaborate, vine-covered, curling black metal before lowering his head as though bowing.

Maeve lingered, unable to see anything but a veil of black where Yddgrasil's roots disappeared. Though the wolf's black fur was matted with blood, his eyes glowed the warm color of a robin's breast and she couldn't hide her curiosity.

"Can I pet him?" she whispered to Hel.

Hel smirked and motioned her forward, sharing an amused glance with Modgud. "How could he say no to a warrior like you?"

Maeve inched closer, reaching a hand out in asking. Garmr's tale wagged like a puppy's as she ran her fingers through his rough fur. It was difficult to believe the teeth poking from his lips had torn Draugr to shreds not so long ago.

"Nice to meet you," she said, growing more confident. Garmr hopped up, resting his paws on Maeve's chest.

"All right," Hel muttered. "Don't get carried away, Garmr."

Garmr licked Maeve's cheeks and then retreated, causing Maeve to giggle.

"This is where we leave you," another voice rumbled behind, putting an end to the playfulness. Hrym's gaze held sorrow, his hand resting on the hilt of his ax. "It seems Hekla has calmed. We have a ship to rebuild back in Jötunheim."

"What about that mead you wanted?" Hel asked, her forehead wrinkling as though disappointed.

"Another time," he promised, holding his hand out.

Hel shook it and then lifted her voice for his crew to hear: "Thank you. All of you. We may not have made it home without you."

"It was a pleasure." Hrym's dark eyes fell to Maeve, and where once she might have squirmed, now she only tilted her head expectantly. "I apologise to you, Skjaldmær. I was wrong. You're as worthy a warrior as any of us, and you make Hel stronger just by being near. It's no mean feat, gaining the love of a goddess. I've certainly tried." He winked and Hel rolled her eyes. "Still, there is always our most esteemed guard of Gjalla—"

"No," Modgud said before he could finish and Maeve had to trap her cackle as she patted Hrym on the shoulder — having to stand on her tiptoes to do so.

"You're forgiven. Thank you, Hrym."

All teasing dissipated as he dipped his head, his features nothing but sincere as he stepped away. "*Vér sjáumst*," he said, and though Maeve didn't understand the words, she knew it was a goodbye — for now. She hoped one day she'd see the faces of the people she fought with again. There was so much to hope for now.

"*Farvel.*" Hel dipped her head and then the crew was ambling away with makeshift spears and weapons in hand, all of them friends now. All of them off for another adventure.

Maeve was content to stay here, in her own.

"Are you ready?" Hel asked, lacing their fingers together.

Maeve nodded, and together, with Helhest following close behind, they entered the blackness.

* * *

The sunlight was blinding. It glinted off everything, bleaching the turrets white and bouncing off the snowy mountains in the distance. It took Maeve a moment to catch her breath. She stood at the end of a winding road, still hand in hand with Hel. Yggdrasil's roots narrowed into the soil beside her, grass and wildflowers growing over the raised earth. Blue sky yawned out for miles, only a little paler than what she was used to. Everywhere, there were thatched roofs and people of all ages, shapes, and sizes milling around, some of them greeting Hel as they passed while others were too busy wandering market stalls or chatting with others.

It wasn't like stepping into the afterlife. It was like stepping into a painting or a scene from a historical movie. There were no Pret A Mangers to ruin this time, no tourists snapping photographs of the bridges. The architecture resembled the stone, fort-like walls of York, offering the feeling of coming home even from realms and oceans away. A man on the edge of a cobbled, narrow street played the lyre, his music tinkling like wind chimes through the hustle and bustle. Everybody seemed happy.

And the castle soared above it all, its spires piercing the wispy clouds, the sun glinting off its windows. Maeve could only assume it was Hel's.

She let go of Hel's hand, stepping forward with a strange, new lightness in her chest. The smell of honeysuckle sweetened the air. A short, round man manning the stall closest greeting her in a language she didn't yet know. A woman ran a jewelry stand beside him and grief fluttered past Maeve like a bird, stopping on her shoulder for a moment as she remembered India. Her jewellery.

But if this was the afterlife, she knew she was safe. That sense, that knowing, curled around Maeve like a blanket.

"Welcome home," whispered Hel.

Maeve smiled. She was certain this place could be just that.

Chapter Seventeen

Hel was exhausted. She'd spent the rest of the day showing Maeve around her castle, allowing her to choose one of the many rooms that suited her. She'd picked a suite just around the corner from Hel's own sleeping quarters — and then followed Hel and promptly fallen asleep on her bed instead.

Hel smiled to herself as she left her bathroom wrapped in a soft towel, her skin flushed and damp from a long, steaming bath. She would fill another for Maeve, soon, but now, she perched on the edge of her bed and looked at her skjaldmær's sprawled, content figure. Maeve's chest rose and fell steadily, her face still blood-spattered and eyelashes flickering against her cheeks. Hel brushed the silver hair from Maeve's face, a tenderness swelling inside her. She could get used to having somebody here with her; somebody as beautiful and utterly unpredictable as Maeve.

She'd never felt the need to before. Being a goddess didn't require a partner, and she'd never found an equal in the warriors she welcomed into her kingdom. Never been particularly interested in looking. Now, it was all she wanted; to lie down with Maeve in this very bed, nestled under the pillows, exploring her all over again until she cried out in pleasure. For the first time in her lifetime, Hel did not walk this world alone.

It was like falling out of the sky and landing on silk and cotton.

Maeve stirred beneath Hel's touch, her lids opened slowly. "What time is it?" she said groggily, and then, rubbing her eyes: "Oh. Wait. Does time exist here?"

Hel shrugged. "We have night and day. Time doesn't determine how we fill the hours between, though."

Maeve's yawn rattled through the bedroom as she snuggled closer to Hel, tracing soft circles into her bare thigh and letting out a content sigh. "So I can have lots of afternoon naps and nobody will judge me?"

Smirking, Hel smoothed her wild hair down, lips aching with the overwhelming need to kiss Maeve raw. She was so strange. Beautiful. Honest. And she'd chosen Hel. She'd never looked more alive than now, as tired as she was, with hooded lids and one cheek pinker than the other from sleeping on it.

"You can have all of the naps anytime you wish," Hel confirmed. "But before you take your next one, perhaps a bath? You are getting dried blood on my sheets."

Maeve hummed. "A bath sounds good." Still, her finger travelled higher, toying with the hem of Hel's towel so that Hel's core began to burn with want. "Perhaps you should stay in this towel while I wash."

"Why is that?"

She smirked lazily, circles getting longer, slower, wider, on the inside of Hel's thigh. "No sense in getting dressed when I'd quite like to do things that involve being *un*dressed."

"Hmm." It was an effort not to turn Maeve over and have her way with her immediately, but she suppressed her lust. There was more she wanted yet. "As lovely as that sounds, I was wondering if I might take you out tonight."

Maeve's circles stopped as she met Hel's gaze expectantly.

She suddenly felt even more bare, exposed. "I promised you a dance. I know we have an eternity now, and I'm sure you're exhausted after today, but… I would like to make more memories with you than just ones of war and battle."

Slowly, Maeve rose to a seat, twirling Hel's damp hair between her fingers. "I'm not tired. I'm wide awake for the first time in my life. You can take me anywhere you want to. The answer will always be yes."

Hel broke into a smile, realizing she'd probably never done it quite so much as since meeting Maeve. It might have been Maeve who was new here, but Hel's own body, her skin, felt like it had been replaced with something altogether brighter. She almost didn't recognize herself without all that darkness lingering like a cloud over her head.

She brought Maeve's hand to her lips, tasting the ash of the day on her skin. She'd been given a second chance. She intended to make the most of every second.

* * *

Hel's clothes were a little bit big for Maeve, so she was currently using one of her shirts as a knee-length dress, sleeves rolled up and her belt fastened to hide all the excess material around her waist.

It smelled like her; like smoke and earth, sea salt and icy winds. She looked at her reflection in the mirror and smiled before slipping on her boots. It was strange, all of it. She felt clean and fresh and well-rested, though not a few hours ago she'd been anything but. There was no make-up to be found in the castle, so her face was clear of the products she usually wore to feel a bit prettier — but then, she didn't seem to need them. Her skin glowed like sunlight, eyes as bright as the sky outside. Everything had changed, and she had never felt more certain that she was where she was supposed to be. She could be happy here.

Just in time, Hel appeared at the doorway in a black tunic and leather trousers, her hair braided across one shoulder. "Ready?"

Maeve was. They left the palace together, a place filled with vast, echoey spaces and paintings on every wall. A week ago, she might have expected the goddess of death to live in shadows, but now, it didn't surprise her that her halls were filled with art and light.

Outside, the town still teemed with excitement, and many eyes fell to them as they entered the heart of it.

"Don't be alarmed if they all flock to you," Hel said. "Modgud has already been telling tales of the skjaldmær who captured Hel's cold, dead heart and brought it back to life."

Maeve warmed, though she shot Hel a sharp look. "Your heart was never dead. It's the warmest one I know."

"Modgud enjoys being dramatic." Hel tugged her closer, greeting those around them as they trundled past market stalls and narrow homes, through families whose eyes lit up when they saw Maeve. Before too long, they were stopping every other step to answer questions about Hel's most recent battle, all of them interested in Maeve and her strange story. Hel always kept Urd and her sisters out of it, never once mentioning the Norns, which was more grace than they deserved — "I won't be the one to tamp out my peoples' faith in them," Hel muttered to her between conversations, only more proof that her heart had beat just fine without Maeve. That much was clear from the way her people spoke to her, respect and admiration shining in their eyes. They loved her, and she them. Maeve was lucky to be the woman who went home with her tonight.

Eventually, they reached a place labeled with a painted sign and Norse letters Maeve could not read. Music floated from inside as well as the sound of laughter.

"You'll have to teach me your language," Maeve said.

"It'll come to you. For now, enjoy the surprise." Hel pushed the arched door open and the honeyed smell of wine and ale wafted out. A pub, not so different from the ones in York. She may as well have been back there, surrounded by cosplayers and reenactors like her.

Excitedly, she stepped in, shifting from foot to foot when more gazes found her.

"Skjaldmær Maeve!" somebody shouted, and then cheers and claps began and Maeve's face burned. They were applauding her... treating her like a hero.

Hel beamed proudly at her side. "That's right. One of the best warriors I have met in a long time — but Maeve is still new here, so let's break her in gently. Tonight, we will drink to Hekla for keeping us safe in difficult times."

More cheers, but they ebbed quickly as Hel ushered her to a booth in the corner. She didn't need to ask; two horns of wine were brought over by a woman not much shorter than Hel. "An honour," she said to Maeve.

"May you ask our musicians to play us a song?" Hel asked. "I'd like to show Maeve how wonderful they sound."

"Of course." The woman scuttled off.

Hel grinned smugly as she took a sip of her wine, wiping her mouth with the back of her hand afterward. Maeve could only rest her elbow on the table, warmth seeping through her. It would be strange for a while, she knew, but hadn't she always hoped for change? Hadn't she always wanted to be looked at the way Hel looked at her? Hadn't she always wanted to feel capable of anything?

The first dulcet notes of what sounded like a harp drifted through the pub, somehow sounding both mournful and sanguine. Another joined in and Maeve searched for the source of the music, finding a band of four, two of whom were sprightly women cradling lyres. Another played something that resembled a piano while a plump man held tinkling bells in each hand.

It happened like a flood; the sound stuttered and tinkled through the pub at first before burbling like a stream, and then eventually swallowing them like waves. It was beautiful, every moment of it. Maeve had never seen such deft fingers, never heard music with so much lingering behind the melody. The musicians told a story without words, and Maeve hung onto every line.

After the first one, Hel offered her hand.

Maeve took it without question, letting the goddess drag her into the centre of the crowd. She put one heavy hand on Maeve's hip, the other clasping her hand. Maeve mirrored her, closing her eyes as serenity took over and she began to sway. "Nobody has ever danced with me before. Not like this."

"What was music like for you?" Hel questioned.

"It depended. There were a lot of genres. Nothing as beautiful as this, really, but I went to a few concerts that were magical." Sadness fought its way up her throat and she let it. It was okay to miss her old life, especially the things she'd never get back. As long as she knew she could be happy here, it was okay. "There was this band called *Fleetwood Mac*. I think you'd like them."

"What instruments did they play?"

"Drums, guitar, a tambourine that sounded a bit like those bells." She nodded at the band still playing. "But Stevie Nicks has a voice that takes you somewhere else."

"I'll put a good word in with the Norns. See if they can get them here," Hel said in a mock whisper, though her smile was solemn, no doubt thinking of Urd and her games.

"What will happen with the Norns? Doesn't anybody regulate this stuff? The gods, maybe?"

"As long as fate serves them well in Asgard, I fear they won't care too much what the Norns do." Hel's mouth tipped into a frown. "I'll figure out a way to make sure this never happens again, but I'd like to hope Urd's sisters know better than to let it."

"They seemed sorry," Maeve agreed.

Hel hummed in thought before that absent film faded from her eyes. She was here again. "Let's not think of them tonight."

"Okay," Maeve breathed, growing closer to Hel as the lyrist plucked out a lamenting solo. She knew people were watching, but she couldn't find it in her to care about anything but the heart thudding against her cheek, the large hand engulfing her own. She'd never felt this safe in somebody else's arms, and not just because the arms in question were roughly the size of stone pillars.

Hel cared about her. She'd brought her home at last after protecting her, promising her that she would. There was nothing Maeve couldn't face now. She'd always thought the idea of immortality boring, but that was before she'd known how different the afterlife could be. She was excited to live out an endless amount of days like this.

Hel's hand fell to the small of Maeve's back, her touch turning gentle. "Is it what you imagined?"

"Even better," Maeve admitted.

Hel placed a kiss in her hair, but it wasn't enough. Maeve tugged away just enough to press her lips to Hel's, getting lost in the movement until they were no longer dancing. It felt just like the first time, like thunder and lightning and tempests, but she could feel the sun peeking through the clouds now, warming her skin.

She cupped Hel's cheeks, one supple, one hard, and knew she would never quite understand how she'd gotten here. Still, thank goodness she had.

"*Ástin mín,*" Hel whispered.

"My love," Maeve replied.

Glossary

Asgard - the home of the Norse gods

Ástin mín - an Icelandic term of endearment meaning "my love"

Draugr - reanimated corpses in Norse mythology

Garmr - a hellhound/wolf who guards the gates of Hel

Gjallarbrú - the bridge that spans the river Gjöll on the road to Hel

Gjöll - a river that must be crossed on the way to Helheim, said to separate the living from the dead

Farvel - a Norse term meaning "goodbye"

Jorvik - the Norse name for York, a historical city in the north of the UK

Jotunheim - a land inhabited by the jötnar

Jötunn - giants (jötnar is plural)

Heill þik - an Old Nose phrase me meaning "hail to you"

Hekla - an Icelandic volcano where the gates of Hel are said to reside

Hel - the Norse goddess of death and the daughter of Loki (also the name of India's beloved cat)

Helheim - an afterlife location ruled by Hel, who receives many of the dead after battle

Helhest - Hel's three-legged horse, nicknamed Hester

Hrym - the jötunn captain of *Naglfar*, also known as Hrymr

Ísland - Iceland

Loki - the trickster god, son of Odin and father of Hel

Midgard - the realm inhabited by humans

Modgud - the guardian of Gjallarbrú

Muspelheim - the realm of fire

The Norns - the Fates, three deities responsible for shaping human destiny named Urd, Skuld, and Verdandi.

Naglfar - a boat said to be made of nails of the dead, foretold to ferry monsters to the gods for war

Niflheim - a realm of ice and cold where those who do not die a heroic death go

Odin - a prominent god who is the father of Thor and Loki

Ragnarök - a series of events that leads to the world's ending and rebirth

Sif - a goddess linked to the earth and married to Thor

Skjaldmær - "shield-maiden," a female warrior from Scandinavian folklore

Valhalla - a hall in Asgard for heroes who die in combat, presided over by Odin

Vér sjáumst - Old Norse phrase meaning "goodbye/see you soon"

Yggdrasil - a giant ash tree at the centre of the universe whose roots branch off to different realms

About the Author

Bryony Rosehurst is a British romance author dedicated to telling diverse stories of love and happily ever afters — and perhaps a little bit of angst sprinkled in for good measure. You can usually find her painting (badly), photographing new cities (occasionally), or wishing for autumn (always). Chat with her on Twitter: @BryonyRosehurst.

Also by Bryony Rosehurst

More queer stories, more happily ever afters…

Love, Anon (Hayes Family, #1)
Christmas is approaching and Arden Hayes is in dire need of a date if only to convince her concerned family that she's moved on from her failed marriage.

Rosie Gladwell is lonely in a city that isn't hers, an ocean away from home, and every date that she's been on ends in disaster. When she comes across an advertisement for someone willing to act as a Christmas date on new social media and dating app, Don't Be a Stranger, she responds in the hopes that she won't have to spend Christmas alone — even if it means spending the night pretending to be in a relationship with a stranger. However, as Rosie and Arden get to know one another, they seem to find an instant, undeniable connection. Is it as real as it feels, or just another act?

Meet Me on St. Patrick's Day (Hayes Family, #2)

Is it just the (bad) luck of the Irish that keeps pushing Brennan and Quinn together, or something more?

Quinn Hayes and Brennan O'Keeffe are nothing more than perfect strangers, but when their paths cross often over the years, always on St. Patrick's Day, they realise that they seem to share a connection they've never been able to find with anyone else. Their personal lives are messy and chaotic and ever-changing in so many ways, but their link always remains the same — until a struggling, troubled Quinn makes a misguided mistake, and as a result, believes she has lost Brennan for good.

Years later, she unknowingly walks into his bar, and their lives become entangled once again, with Quinn landing a bartending job as Brennan's co-worker at Irish pub, O'Keeffe's. Will they finally get it right this time, or will Brennan's secrets and Quinn's shadowy past ruin everything once and for all?

On Common Ground (Hayes Family, #3)

World famous fashion designer Francesca Halliday always has somewhere to be, but when her private jet is forced to make an emergency landing due to an unexpected storm, she becomes stranded in the middle of the Scottish Highlands with the pilot, who is none other than Tristan Hayes, an old flame she never planned to see again.

Tristan is fresh out of his divorce and rattled by the reappearance of his ex-ex-ex-girlfriend, especially considering that he never got closure from their sudden break-up nine years ago. Stuck in the middle of nowhere in a terrible storm, will he finally understand the reason why Francesca left him behind to pursue her career, or will facing old wounds only put them more at odds with each other?

Cursed in Love

Ophelia is cursed. Ever since finding an old relic known as Eilidh's ring in the Scottish Highlands three years ago, rumoured to have belonged to a woman once scorned by an unfaithful lover, her love life has been on a downward spiral. When the opportunity comes to return the ring back to its resting place with its namesake, Ophelia seizes it with both hands in the hopes the curse will be lifted. However, when nervy, short-tempered, workaholic Luce is accidentally dragged into her antics (as well as down a couple of waterfalls) during Ophelia's attempt to commandeer her canoe, lifting the curse proves more difficult than planned — particularly with two con men trailing them in the hopes of getting their hands on a precious rare stone embedded within the relic.

With no way of getting Luce back to the campsite she'd been unwillingly holidaying in, where both her anxiety medication and comfort zone reside, she and Ophelia find themselves reluctant allies in their separate attempts to find peace. But hiking through the Hebrides in the middle of winter causes plenty of problems, and with the thieves closing in on Ophelia, tensions run high and feelings begin to develop. Will Luce and Ophelia find common ground and reveal themselves to one another as they work to get the ring back to the lake in which it was found, or will Ophelia be bound to the same tragic fate as Eilidh for the rest of her life?

First Comes Marriage

Impulsive rock star Charlie Dean isn't interested in relationships, let alone marriage, but when her reputation takes a dive after an onstage meltdown, she runs out of options to repair her image. With her manager signing her up for reality TV show, *First Comes Marriage*, where celebrities are matched together and meet for the first time at the altar, she is forced into cleaning up her act once and for all. The problem? Her wife is none other than Tamara Hewitt, a glamorous plus-size model who Charlie could never possibly be compatible with.

At least, so she believes. Tamara and Charlie come to an agreement, accepting that in order to get through the next six to twelve weeks of newlywed challenges and come out of the other side loved by the public again, they must play up to the cameras — but will they fake it till they make it, or is an arranged marriage between two women from very separate worlds doomed to end in tragedy?

Perfect for fans of *Married at First Sight*.

When Love Barges In

Piper Stevens has always been intimidated by best friend Max Lockett's older sister, Jamie, despite having been practically taken in by the Lockett family from the age of fourteen. Given her rough past in foster care, her altogether shy and nervous disposition, and a tiny crush on the openly queer woman that caused Piper to come to terms with her own sexuality, things have always been awkward between them.

After two years of traveling, Jamie is back in their small town of Hebden Bridge, and seeing Piper again brings back old feelings — as well as new ones. Jamie has never understood the uneasiness between them, and she resented the way it made her feel out of place in her own home, but they're both willing to try to be friendlier for Max's benefit. When Piper agrees to model for Jamie's plus-size handmade clothing line, it soon becomes clear that the tension between them stems from more than just awkwardness. But can they allow themselves to finally fall for one another, or will their mutual loyalty to Max keep them apart?

Running with the Wolf

Journey alongside Beatrice Blackstone as she embarks on a thrilling adventure, discovering her extraordinary abilities and the shocking truth about her past.

For years, Beatrice believed she was an ordinary girl. But when her first vision exposes a haunting premonition of death, everything changes. Her world is shattered, and she learns that she is no ordinary girl at all – she is a witch. With her coven under relentless pursuit by hunters, Beatrice must navigate the perilous path of her newfound powers. And she won't face it alone.

Enter Leighton Myers, a fierce werewolf and a skilled bodyguard-for-hire. Drawn together by fate, Beatrice and Leighton forge an unlikely alliance, their lives intertwined in a dangerous dance. With Leighton's strength and expertise, Beatrice finds solace in her protection. Yet, beneath Leighton's steadfast facade lies a secret that could unravel everything they hold dear.

As they crisscross the enchanting landscapes of Europe, their journey becomes a breathtaking chase against time. Every step brings them closer to the truth behind Beatrice's coven and the sinister forces determined to extinguish their magic forever. But amidst the adrenaline-fueled pursuit, a forbidden connection blossoms between Beatrice and Leighton. Will their growing bond prove to be their salvation or a fatal distraction?

"Running with the Wolf" is a spellbinding tale that combines heart-stopping action, spine-tingling magic, and a breathtaking romance. Lose yourself in a world where danger lurks at every turn, where witches and werewolves collide, and where love may be the greatest magic of all. Join Beatrice Blackstone on her extraordinary journey and discover that sometimes, the most incredible adventures begin when we embrace the power within.

Printed in Great Britain
by Amazon

31955104R00091